"I'm going for a swim. Why don't you join me?"

Alex stayed where she was. Cole wasn't wearing briefs, and though she'd been to bed with him any number of times, the sight of him standing fully, gloriously naked in broad daylight caught her off guard.

Shrugging at her reticence, he climbed over the rocks and lowered himself into the lagoon. Then he dived under and reemerged a few seconds later, water dripping down his face, his broad shoulders, his lean torso...

He seemed to sense the direction of her thoughts. "I want you, Alex. I want you to come to me as bare as the day you were born."

Alex hesitated. This was their last day together in Belize. Why not make it memorable?

She pulled the peasant blouse over her head, then kicked off her sandals. Knowing that his eyes followed her every move, she forced herself to slow down.

When she stepped out of her skirt, Cole's jaw dropped. "All this time you've been riding around without underwear? Do you know how turned on that makes me?"

Noticing his erection, Alex gave a soft laugh. "I think I've got a pretty good idea...."

Dear Reader,

I've always been a sucker for a good reunion love story. Clichéd as it may sound, love truly can be sweeter the second time around, especially when the universe grants us a chance to reconnect with The One Who Got Away.

In *Every Breath You Take...* microbiologist Alexandra—Alex—Kendall and FBI special agent Cole Whittaker meet, fall in love, then lose each other through no fault of their own. Flash forward five years. Biotechnologies mogul Randall Traxton, Alex's boss and fiancé, hires Cole to be her up-close-and-personal bodyguard on a treacherous mission to Belize. Jetting from Manhattan to the steamy Caribbean, can these two formerly star-crossed lovers surrender the painful past and trust enough to fall in love again?

Wishing you a 2009 filled with sexy second chances and bright new beginnings,

Hope Tarr
www.hopetarr.com

Hope Tarr

EVERY BREATH YOU TAKE...

HARLEQUIN®

TORONTO • NEW YORK • LONDON
AMSTERDAM • PARIS • SYDNEY • HAMBURG
STOCKHOLM • ATHENS • TOKYO • MILAN • MADRID
PRAGUE • WARSAW • BUDAPEST • AUCKLAND

Recycling programs
for this product may
not exist in your area.

ISBN-13: 978-0-373-79445-4
ISBN-10:   0-373-79445-2

EVERY BREATH YOU TAKE…

ABOUT THE AUTHOR

Hope Tarr is an award-winning author of multiple contemporary and historical category and single-title romance novels. Every Breath You Take... is her fifth contribution to Harlequin's supersexy Blaze line and her first manuscript to be written from her new home, New York City. To enter Hope's monthly contest or check out the latest news on her "semi blog," visit her online at www.hopetarr.com.

Books by Hope Tarr

HARLEQUIN BLAZE
293—IT'S A WONDERFULLY SEXY LIFE
317—THE HAUNTING
364—STROKES OF MIDNIGHT
407—BOUND TO PLEASE

Don't miss any of our special offers. Write to us at the following address for information on our newest releases.

Harlequin Reader Service
U.S.: 3010 Walden Ave., P.O. Box 1325, Buffalo, NY 14269
Canadian: P.O. Box 609, Fort Erie, Ont. L2A 5X3

For my editor, Brenda Chin,
with friendship and thanks.

Acknowledgments

My appreciation goes out to Eric Ammon, formerly
of Jets.com, for patiently answering my questions
about private jet travel—and then just as patiently
supplying the information I needed but didn't know
enough to ask. Also, to Barb S in the Customer
Response Center of 3M Industrial & Transportation
Business for her superspeedy reply to my frantic
e-mail on how to remove duct tape. Barb, you're an
angel and a lifesaver.

To my friends and fellow authors: Lisa Arlt for
generously sharing her firsthand knowledge of
Belize based on her family's former residence there
and Terri Ridgell for keeping me honest on the
science aspects of the book. Any errors that may
have found their way into these pages are,
of course, entirely my own.

Finally to my friends Mike and Lisa Davila
for turning me, and by extension my fictional
characters, on to Zabar's, the ultimate
New York gourmet grocery experience.
Oy vey, and God bless!

Prologue

Denver, Colorado, 2003

FBI SPECIAL AGENT Cole Whittaker, known by his current cover, country-and-western crooner Cole Calhoun, smiled over at the very special lady lying tucked up in his arms. "Happy?"

Alexandra Kendall—Alex—took a break from tracing the bracelet tattoo banding his biceps and lifted her head of wavy blond hair from his pillow. "Do you even have to ask?"

Like the tattoo, their chance meeting a month ago in the smoky bar in the city's trendy LoDo District was permanently etched on his being. Looking down from the stage where he was playing lead guitar and belting out the final refrain to "American Pie," he spotted a trio of young women pushing their way toward the front. The feather boas flung across their ski jackets and glitter glued to their cheeks proclaimed their night out to be a party occasion. He zeroed in on the third woman, the blonde, and what breath he had left at the end of an eight-minutes-plus classic rock song seized up in his lungs. She wore a paper party tiara with the number 30 embossed in sparkles and a shyer version of her friends' broad grins. No glitter on it, but her lovely oval face gave off a definite glow. She peeled off her heavy ski jacket and Cole forgot to breathe. The cable-knit sweater and boot-cut jeans were standard winter wear, but on her they suggested a slender athletic body graced with subtle curves. She must have sensed him staring. Suddenly she stopped talking to her friends and looked up at the stage. Her gaze connected with his, and Cole felt something powerful and alien slam into him, a cross between a shot to the heart and a sucker punch to the gut.

Damn! His perfect lady had walked into his life at the worst possible time. The bar was a hang-out for the leadership of a Denver-based militia group known as the Sons of Saul. The Feds had been monitoring the group for nearly a year, but in the post-Waco and Ruby Ridge law-enforcement world, caution was everyone's watchword. Recent intelligence reports indicated the group had begun recruiting from outside the state. That and a connection to at least one international terrorist group warranted intervention. Cole had spent the past several months undercover posing as the leader of a country-and-western band. Like him, his fellow band members were all federal agents who'd dabbled in popular music over the years. Feed the crowd classics like "Mustang Sally," "American Pie," and "Ring of Fire" with the occasional dance tune thrown in, and you were golden.

That Alex lived and worked in Philly teaching high school biology allowed him to keep up the deception. The four short weekends they'd so far shared had been filled with hot sex and long walks, stimulating conversations and companionable silences. They'd even broached the subject of kids, tiptoeing around the issue, feeling each other out. It turned out they both wanted a bunch. He could only hope that once he came clean with her and revealed his identity as a sniper on the FBI's elite Hostage Rescue Team, whatever feelings she had for him would be strong enough for her to forgive the lie—and still consider a future together.

Because he didn't want just to be with her in the moment, as amazing as those moments were. He wanted to make plans with her and make babies with her and live to grow middle-aged and finally old with her. The growing-old part didn't jibe with his job description. As an FBI field operative, you woke up each morning never knowing if that day might be your last. He'd never made promises to a woman before, both because he'd never found the right woman to make them to, and because he'd always assumed he didn't have all that much to give.

But Alex was different, and when he was with her, he was different, too, more himself than he'd ever been. Beyond concealing what he did for a living, the Big Lie as he'd started thinking of it, he hadn't held back. Excluding his mother, she was probably the only person on earth who knew that any food prepared with peanut oil made him break out in hives or that the small white scar on his forehead came not from any daredevil deed but from his baby brother bashing him on the head with the jagged edge of an opened soup can.

In another couple of hours he'd get up, dig his truck out from the latest snowstorm and drive her to the airport to catch her flight. But as soon as the mission wrapped, in the next few weeks, he hoped, he'd come clean with her. And afterward, assuming she didn't knee him in the nuts and walk away, he'd ask her to be his wife.

She leaned over and pressed a soft kiss onto his shoulder. "I can't imagine being like this with anyone else."

Cole didn't answer. What he wanted to say—make that shout to the rooftops—was along the lines of, "I love you. Marry me," but with the mission in full swing and him still in deep cover, how could he? He was a man of action, not words, and a marriage proposal was too monumental a moment in a woman's life to risk messing up.

Instead he eased her down on her back, covering her long, slender body with his, and her mouth and jaw and neck with his kisses.

She framed his jaw with her elegant, long-fingered hands. The love in the honey-brown eyes gazing up into his had his heart fisting. "Cole, I—"

"Shhh, baby..."

He laid a finger across her cool lips and looked deeply into her eyes and prayed she'd look back into his just as deeply, long enough to see the love he was so desperately trying to show her. And even as he made love to her in near silence, inside his chest the trapped words pounded to be released.

I love you, Lex.

The future would take care of itself. He had to believe that. He had to.

1

"TELL ME, Mr. Whittaker, what must I do to have you?" Randall Traxton, founder and CEO of Traxton Biotechnologies, Inc., turned away from the bank of floor-to-ceiling glass windows overlooking Madison Square Park, his steely stare striking Cole like a bullet between the eyes.

Standing on the other side of Traxton's glass-topped desk with hands folded behind his back, Cole let the question hang in the expensively filtered air. Ordinarily he would have appreciated, even admired, Traxton's directness. He'd never had much patience for shooting the bull, and riding the red-eye from Denver, even if his potential client had booked him into first-class, hadn't increased his inclination toward sociability.

Beyond the CEO's pin-striped shoulder lay the panorama of Manhattan skyline. Cole had never been a big "I love New York" guy, but he had to admit the view was spectacular. From a security standpoint, though, all that glass made Traxton an easy target. A sniper on stake-out would have a bird's-eye bead on the back of the CEO's immaculately coiffed dark head. Bang-bang! Cold zero! Gotcha!

Two years ago, Cole had joined with four other security

professionals and set up shop as Guidepost International, a private security firm specializing in executive escort, asset protection and site security. Since nine-eleven, firms like his were cropping up like clover, but few if any of his competitors could match the collective expertise of the A-list team he'd amassed. He and his four partners, Mike, Sal, Lester and Jake, had successfully managed every domestic and international crisis involving U.S. citizens that had come their way over the past decade. Escorting one of Traxton's executives to Belize and back was meat-and-potatoes stuff. So why was Traxton so insistent that Cole staff the four-day trip personally?

Ever since he'd stepped inside the lavishly appointed art-deco office ten minutes before, Cole's bullshit barometer had shot to red alert. Traxton was withholding information about the assignment; Cole would bet his former badge on it.

Fortunately, silence wasn't only the oldest interrogation technique in the book, it was also the easiest to apply. The unrelenting quiet made most people so uncomfortable that oftentimes they confessed just to fill the void.

Predictably Traxton began to fidget, turning the band of his flashy gold watch around and around. "Well, Mr. Whittaker?"

"Any of my four associates will be more than capable of handling the assignment. I'm not available."

"And yet you're here."

"To meet with you and spec out the mission parameters—period."

But there was more to his refusal than needing to hold the line on his travel. He didn't like Traxton. As an FBI field agent, he'd dealt with his share of egotistical assholes. The private sector didn't have a premium on pricks. And yet something about Traxton poked at him.

He mentally ran through the results of the preliminary

background check he'd run on the CEO before accepting his invitation to a face-to-face. Born and bred in rural Pennsylvania to a family of dairy farmers, a bachelor's in Business Administration from Harvard. He'd dropped out of his last year in Harvard Law, which begged the question why. No kids, at least not legitimate ones. Never married, which, considering his age and position, was a little weird. Most guys playing at Traxton's level had the requisite wife on board to mug for the cameras and run their social calendars. Had there been a Mrs. Traxton, she would be a decade younger, a thirty-something blond socialite who favored expensive sweater sets and pearl chokers, absolutely "adored" tennis, especially if the club pro sported six-pack abs, and was on the board of any number of "worthy causes."

"Before I can answer yes or no I need to be clear on why you're sending your executive to Belize, what you expect him to accomplish there, and the nature of any anticipated threat."

Traxton's gaze veered away. "Of course, of course, but first won't you have a seat?" He gestured with one soft white hand toward a pair of scrupulously restored low-backed art-deco chairs in buttery soft leather and maple veneer.

Cole shook his head. "I'm fine standing, thanks."

After being captured in planes and airports for six solid hours, closer to eight counting the layover in Houston, Traxton could have offered him a throne, and Cole still would have turned it down. As soon as this meeting was over, he'd head back to the Roosevelt Hotel, go for a run and then order up room service before crashing in the king-size bed. He could look forward to a decadent six hours of sleep, twice the *zees* he normally logged in per night, before he had to get up and head for the airport and home, though his empty townhouse hardly seemed that. Other than a potted fern he forgot to water more often than he remembered, nothing and no one waited.

For a blink of time five years ago—make that one fairy-tale perfect month—he'd thought his life might turn out very differently. He'd imagined himself coming home to a house that was boisterous and busy. He'd imagined himself coming home to Alex. Even after five years of absolutely no contact, the memories cropped up at the oddest, most inconvenient times. To cope, he stayed as nonstop busy as a body could, short of crashing. If he ever caught up on his sleep, there'd be hell to pay.

Traxton broke the silence. "Six months ago Belize discovered a new and potentially very profitable natural resource. Unfortunately for the Belizeans, their country lacks the infrastructure and funds to develop and market the resulting product effectively. After soliciting proposals from a dozen biotechnologies firms in the U.S., Canada and Western Europe, the government culled the competition to two finalists, Traxton Biotech and our San Francisco-based rival, Sun Coast Biotechnical Laboratories. My Director of Research and Development is headed to Belize to make our final presentation to the Prime Minister and cabinet. Sun Coast Biotech, our competitor, will also have a representative there."

Cole mentally ran through what he knew about Belize, wondering what natural resource might be of interest to a biotech firm. There'd been some recent discoveries of petroleum deposits in the country's Cayo and Toledo districts, but so far the yield had been modest. Regardless, Traxton wasn't in the oil business. Sugar accounted for almost half of the country's exports, and the banana industry was the largest employer, at least officially. Unofficially, a growing involvement in the South American drug trade was a source of U.S. concern.

Illegal drugs had taken Cole to Belize seven years ago, albeit in a roundabout way. As a sniper on the Hostage Rescue Team, he'd spent three grueling weeks staking out a drug lord's jungle compound where the son of a Texas oil tycoon was being held for ransom. The kid, who'd come to Belize on a backpacking trip with some college buddies, had wandered beyond the main tourist area in Belize City and been snatched. When he didn't show up at the designated meet-up spot, his friends contacted the U.S. consul. The HRT had gotten the young man out unhurt, though the drug lord hadn't fared so well. Still, Belize was politically stable, English-speaking, and about as safe for westerners as the Developing World got. So long as visitors kept to the main streets and stayed in reputable resorts, they should be fine.

"You should know up front that if you're using your company as a cover for organized crime, anything illegal, our association ends here."

"Organized crime! What a vivid imagination you have, Mr. Whittaker. You really should try your hand at novel writing."

Cole felt a sharp fisting in the vicinity of his heart. Five years ago, Alex had been working on a novel. He wondered if she'd ever finished it and found a publisher. Unless she wrote under a pen name, he could find out easily enough—the information would be only a mouse click away—but not checking was part of the deal he'd made with himself to leave her be.

"At the end of four days, the Belizean cabinet will cast its definitive vote on which firm will receive the sole source contract to develop and market the…resource. The result of the vote will be announced at a banquet on the final night. The

Belizean government will, of course, provide its own security for all scheduled events. Hiring outside protection is likely unnecessary, but I've never been a man who welcomes surprises."

Cole understood completely. Hiring a bodyguard was often more about enhancing prestige than needing actual protection. Unless the principal was an A-list celebrity stalked by a fanatical fan or a high-profile tycoon in danger of being kidnapped for ransom, there usually wasn't much cause for worry. Movies and television to the contrary, not all that many people were important enough to attract targeted violence.

"You want the flash of your boy walking into the negotiations with a professional bullet catcher in tow, fair enough. But why fly me out here when there are at least a dozen comparable in-state security companies that offer travel escort?"

Traxton didn't hesitate, didn't miss a goddamned beat. "I don't settle for mediocre, Mr. Whittaker. Your professional reputation precedes you. You spent a decade in the FBI working virtually every high-profile domestic case to cross the news monitor. Your last assignment earned you the Agency's Medal of Honor."

Behind his back, Cole fisted his folded hands. His actions during the six-week siege of the Sons of Saul compound had won him the coveted honor, but his being there had lost him the woman he loved. It had lost him Alex. He'd ended up tossing the medal in the trash.

"Your record of service is more than unblemished. It's stellar."

Try expunged. Even after five years, he felt the old rancor burn like bile.

Traxton cocked his head and regarded him. "I'm curious as to why you chose to leave the Agency at the pinnacle of your career? Walking away from an FBI pension is all but unheard of."

It was a reasonable question and far from the first time he'd been asked. And yet coming as it did from Traxton, Cole felt himself bristling. "Would you believe I was feeling entrepreneurial?"

The break-up with Alex had wrecked him. If he could go back for a redo, he'd take his team leader up on his offer of two weeks' leave and use the time to get his shit together. Instead, he'd tried to be a tough guy and act like losing the woman he loved was no big deal. Looking back, he saw he'd been a walking time bomb, a loose cannon. Angry at the Agency but mostly at himself, he'd let some gang punk goad him into firing his weapon without authorization or backup.

These days, the government could export terrorist suspects to foreign countries for "interrogation," but a law-enforcement officer discharging his sidepiece improperly on U.S. soil brought the press raining down like locusts. Had he hung on, the Internal Affairs investigation would have severed his "stellar" career as surely as a bullet striking bone.

Shaking himself back to the present, Cole said, "Mike Stevens, one of my principals, is a former Chicago police commander. Your VP will be in good hands."

Traxton frowned. "I believe I've made it clear I want you." His voice wasn't particularly deep, but the tone was firm.

Cole shook his head. "I don't go into the field much these days. Unless the mission specifications warrant my direct involvement, my associates cover the hands-on operations."

Between them, Mike, Sal, Lester and Jake boasted a résumé of expertise in high-speed evasive driving, explosives detection, surveillance and counter-surveillance and threat analysis. Cole was a crack sniper and evasive driver, but he was also the only one among them with a business degree. That made him the logical choice to head up the financial end of the operation. Steering Guidepost to the next level meant spending more time as a CEO and less as an operative. How ironic was it that he'd left the Agency to avoid being warehoused in an administrative desk job, and yet these days writing proposals and business briefs and scoping out new projects was more or less all he did? Still, ferrying some white-bread senior exec around Belize's casinos, golf courses and beaches wasn't exactly how he envisioned getting his action fix.

The CEO's smile never slipped, but a telltale crease appeared dead center in his otherwise baby-smooth forehead. Botox? Cole wondered. At thirty-nine, he was nearly a decade younger than Traxton, but his face was starting to resemble a roadmap thanks to ten years' exposure to the elements while on stakeout and a lifetime of too little sleep.

"Mr. Whittaker, I'm prepared to pay you a great deal of money, triple your already exorbitant fee plus expenses, to have you personally staff this mission. Surely that merits your making an exception."

The man's hubris was as off the charts as his investment portfolio. Cole briefly considered walking out, but he'd learned the hard way that it didn't pay to be a loose cannon. Eventually the inevitable happened. You blew. Traxton was an egotistical asshole, no doubt about it, but dealing with his type was a big part of Cole's job description.

Guidepost was careening toward a crossroads. Mike and Sal wanted to branch out into global securities and see how big they could grow. Les and Jake wanted to keep the operation small, boutique and focused on executive protection. The deciding vote was Cole's. The organization's future depended more on what kinds of contracts he lined up in the next few months. Regardless of which direction he took, the cachet of adding a firm from Fortune 500's top one hundred to Guidepost's corporate client list would be a huge coup. So why was he hesitating? He couldn't afford to turn Traxton down. His back was to the wall—maybe not a glass wall, but a wall all the same.

"Before we go any further, I'm going to need to know just what kind of natural resource we're talking about. If it's not illegal, and the competition is sanctioned by the Belizean government, then you shouldn't have any difficulty telling me what it is in general terms."

Traxton's gaze shuttered. "The operations of Traxton Biotech are none of your business."

"On the contrary, Traxton, if you hire me, your business *is* my business."

Traxton threw back his dark head and laughed. Unlike Cole, who'd started going gray in his early twenties, he showed only a few silver strands at the temples. The rest of his hair was inky black. Cole suspected he colored it along with applying large quantities of mousse. It looked as sculpted and artificial as the rest of him.

"I like you, Mr. Whittaker. Do you know why?"

Cole locked onto Traxton's glittering gaze. "I have no idea."

"Because you are who you are, without pretense or false modesty. I more than suspect you've done dark, deadly deeds that have pushed the envelope on ethics, but you've done them for the right reasons and without apology. My Amish grandmother used to say that a clear conscience makes for a soft pillow. Tell me, Mr. Whittaker, how do you sleep?"

"Like the dead. What about you, Traxton?"

"Like a baby, Mr. Whittaker. Like a fucking newborn."

Denver Airport, 2003

COLE DROVE toward the airport, his windshield wipers doing double time against the falling snow as he sang along with the radio. Alex's plane was due in just a few minutes. Fortunately her flight out of Philly had managed to stay just ahead of the storm. Once he got her back to his place, being snowed in wouldn't be such a bad thing.

For what must be the hundredth time since he'd gotten into the car, he patted the inside pocket of his down vest, making sure the small velvet-covered box holding the Tiffany-set diamond engagement ring hadn't slipped out. Ever since dropping Alex off at the airport last weekend, he'd been seized with the gut-wrenching certainty he wouldn't be seeing her again for a very long while, which was crazy, of course. They'd only known each other five weeks, but each weekend rendezvous was better than the last. When he was with her he could be completely himself, except, of course, when he couldn't. Fortunately she was so sweet, so trusting she took everything he said at face value, including the necessary lies. And yet the black cloud had persisted, following him throughout the week until the other day when he'd found himself standing inside a jewelry store staring into a glass case with a dark velvet lining and loaded with diamond rings. For tonight he'd reserved a booth at the Broker, Denver's finest downtown restaurant. Alex loved it there. He'd taken her there for their first date, and it would be the perfect spot to propose. How ironic that he, who'd been accused of commitment phobia by many a frustrated girlfriend over the years, couldn't wait to get his ring on this woman's finger. He still couldn't reveal his identity until the mission wrapped, but once he did, he hoped she'd be as willing to sign up for becoming Alex Whittaker as she would Alex Calhoun.

His cell phone's pulsing pulled his attention back to the present. Thinking Alex must have landed earlier than scheduled, he grabbed it out of the cup holder and flipped open the case.

The triple digit code on the phone's digital face was like an avalanche of snow burying his dreams. As any HRT operative knew, that flashing triad of numbers meant you were to report to base camp pronto. Non-secure communication was on immediate and strict lock-down, no personal phone calls, text messages, or e-mails, either outgoing or incoming.

"Fuck, fuck, *fuck!*" Cole slammed the side of his hand down on the steering wheel, hard enough for it to hurt.

The next exit coming up was for the airport. He was close, so damned close. How bad would it be for him to park in the hourly lot, run in and find Alex, feed her some bullshit excuse and put her on the next plane back to Philly? The answer was bad, really bad. Discovery could cost him his coveted position on the team. Worse still, if his cover was blown and Alex was seen with him, he could be putting her life in jeopardy.

His foot edged toward the brake, and then settled atop it, slowing the truck down. He flashed his right-turn signal and pulled off at the exit. He'd just gotten back on the interstate in the reverse direction when his phone went off again, belting out the first few bars to Van Morrison's "Brown-Eyed Girl," the song he'd chosen as Alex's signature ring tone.

Clenching the steering wheel with both hands, Cole kept his eyes on the road ahead and drove on.

ALEX STOOD at the gate, scanning the terminal for Cole and gnawing at her nails. Her plane had landed forty-five minutes ago but there was still no sign of Cole. He was always so punctual, more likely to be early than not. Since calling ahead to tell him she was on the ground, she'd called two more times. She didn't want to be a pest, but she was starting to get worried. Who was she kidding? She was already there and quickly escalating to panic. Where was he!

He must be tied up in traffic. It was the only explanation her mind would allow. A snowstorm was a snowstorm even if this was Denver. She shifted her backpack to the opposite shoulder and made a mental note to look into buying some actual luggage before her next weekend visit. Fortunately the pack was light, mostly stuffed with Victoria's Secret lingerie and her black knit special occasion dress for tonight's dinner out. Last night over the phone he'd said he had something really important to say to her, something that couldn't wait. Ordinarily a guy wanting to talk signaled nothing but bad news, but in this case the smile in his voice had her hoping that the super-important thing he had to say to her involved them moving in together or maybe even…marrying. Either way, she'd move out to Denver in a heartbeat. True, they'd only known each other a month—okay, five weeks—but at thirty she'd kissed enough frogs to know that when it was right, it wasn't just right. It was perfect.

Cole Calhoun was The One.

Only now she was stuck alone at the airport in a snowstorm, her would-be fiction writer's mind conjuring nightmare images of car wrecks and avalanches and myriad other disasters to rival anything she'd seen in B-movies as a kid. Looking out the bank of windows to the blizzard going on beyond the glass, she was struck with the sudden, terrible sensation that she wouldn't be seeing Cole, not this weekend and quite possibly not any other.

Dear God, please let him be okay, let him be okay, let him…

Hands shaking, she offloaded her pack, unzipped the outside pocket, and pulled out her cell. Phone in hand, she started punching numbers.

2

"I'M NOT no baby!"

The impassioned declaration coming from the fenced-in playground jarred Alex out of the five-year-old memory and back to the present. Seeing the toddler scooped up and dusted off by his mom, she relaxed against the bench. A tumble from a jungle gym was an early lesson that life wasn't all cupcakes and daisies, but fortunately in this case the fallout looked to be limited to a skinned knee. Watching the young mom's tummy tickle transform the little boy's teary-eyed frown into a smile and then a delighted squeal, Alex felt her heart twist. Such was the magic of motherhood. With any luck in another year or so she'd finally be a mom herself, a rookie member of the stroller brigade.

By this time next month she'd be Mrs. Randall Traxton.

At first she'd had some reservations—okay, *a lot*. The gaps between them in age, money and taste were pretty major if not unbridgeable. At times she found his intellectualism to be tiresome, his insistence on listening only to classical music annoyingly effete—not to mention that after five years and counting she was still hung up on another man, who happened to be his polar opposite. Cole Calhoun, the country-and-western musician who five years ago had swept her off her feet—and then tossed her to the curb.

But at thirty-five her biological clock was ticking toward countdown. Her body still did its monthly thing like clockwork, but time had a way of getting away from a person. She had a window of opportunity, but once it was closed, it would be closed for good. If she wanted children, there was no more time to waste waiting for some perfect prince to happen along.

The telephone conversation last week with her mother had clinched her decision.

You can't go on grieving forever, Alex.

I know, Mom, but—

No buts. What you're waiting for doesn't exist. It just doesn't. Life isn't a fairy tale. There are no princes out there, or princesses, either. We're all frogs, we all have warts. The best any of us can hope for is to find a fellow frog that will care for us, warts and all. This Randall of yours sounds like a good man. From the little you've told me, you're already fond of him. And he has money, he can take care of you, and that means a lot. Why not be grateful for those things and trust that in time love will come?

After a night of sleepless soul-searching, Alex had walked into Randall's office first thing the next morning, interrupted his overseas conference call, and accepted his proposal. He'd been delighted and a touch smug, but then he hadn't gotten where he was in life by taking no for an answer. He'd insisted on opening a bottle of Veuve Clicquot even though it wasn't yet 9:00 a.m. Standing at his office's glass wall, touching her flute to his and looking down onto the park, Alex had felt almost happy. Randall might not fit her girlish vision of Prince Charming, but that didn't mean she couldn't have the rest of the fairy tale. Maybe her life was going to work out after all.

And yet when she'd closed her tired eyes that night, Randall's head resting on the pillow next to hers, the chiseled features looking back at her didn't belong to her fiancé but to a certain country-and-western musician with ice-blue eyes and wavy brown hair threaded with silver.

But she couldn't think about that now. Reality presented more pressing problems than a five-year-old case of unrequited love. Eight months earlier, some Belizean divers had come across a previously undiscovered blue hole, an underwater sinkhole off the coast. Soil and water samples from the site revealed a previously unknown strain of bacteria capable of targeting and digesting the hydrocarbons in petroleum without compromising the existing natural environment. If properly developed, the "smart bacteria" would be a landmark discovery, revolutionizing the way not only the U.S. but companies and governments around the globe approached bioremediation.

Recognizing a potentially very lucrative export, the Belizean government had invited a dozen or so Western biotechnologies firms, including Traxton, to submit proposals for the sole right to develop and merchandize the bacteria on the global market. As Director of Research and Development, Alex had taken the lead on authoring Traxton's comprehensive response. Now, after six months of grueling late nights that frequently morphed into crack-of-dawn mornings, her team's hard work and diligence had paid off. The field had winnowed to two firms: Traxton and their San Francisco based rival, Sun Coast Biotech. The Belizean government had invited both firms to come and make their final presentations to the Prime Minister and cabinet. Alex was scheduled to leave for Belize next Tuesday. When she returned to New York on Friday, she hoped to do so with a signed contract in hand. Even with the substantial Phase I front-loaded development costs factored in, profits over the first five years were projected to be in the billions. Unfortunately, the *Exxon Valdez* oil spill in 1989 wasn't an isolated incident. Such catastrophes were a fact of postmodern life. Once developed, the smart bacteria would be in continuous demand, the customer base encompassing U.S. and foreign governments, environmental groups, petroleum consumers and yes, even oil companies wanting to go green.

Everything had been going great until last week when she'd walked into work and found the anonymous note on her desk.

Go to Belize and you're dead.

Predictably the incident had caused a huge uproar. If she could do things over, she'd throw the thing away and say nothing to anyone, especially Randall. At first he'd insisted on sending someone in her place, but she'd refused to accept that, refused to back down, refused to take no for an answer. The Belize deal was her baby. No one, absolutely no one, came close to knowing the ins and outs of the project like she did. On a personal level, closing it would be her last corporate hurrah before she stepped aside and joined the Hamptons set. She'd be damned if she let some corporate coward with a flair for drama and a certifiable nasty streak steal her glory moment.

In the end, they struck a compromise. He would allow her to go as planned provided she agreed to a bodyguard accompanying her. He had the very man in mind, a former sniper on the FBI's elite Hostage Rescue Team named Whittaker.

Alex had never heard of the guy, and so far she hadn't found the time or interest to run a Google search on him. As much as she balked at being tied to the side of some knuckle dragger for four days, she knew Randall wouldn't let her go unless she agreed. She had. So long as Mr. Whittaker didn't get in her way, she supposed she could cope. "Retired" must mean he was an older gentleman, probably close to her dad's age, not that it mattered. What mattered was her trip was on. She was going to Belize.

Her BlackBerry's beeping signaled the end of her sojourn. With a sigh, she dug into her Kate Spade tote, fished out the device and shut off the alarm. She polished off the last bite of her street-vendor hot dog and wiped her fingers on the thin paper napkin, careful not to get mustard on her beige cashmere coat. Gathering up her trash, she got up to go. She'd promised Randall she'd meet the man, and she knew better than to go back on her word. In this case, he really wasn't asking all that much. All she had to do was stop by his office, walk Mr. Whittaker through the trip agenda—and tactfully but firmly communicate that once they touched down in Belize, she expected him to stay the hell out of her way.

TRAXTON TAPPED two fingers against his smoothly shaven jaw. Standing on the other side of the desk, Cole spotted the sheen of clear nail polish. The guy was a first-class pansy.

"My Director of Research and Development is female— and my fiancée. I could prevent her going, of course, but the fact is she knows the details of our proposal better than anyone. She should. She wrote it. On a personal note, if I held her back, my after-hours life would become a living hell."

So the CEO was pussy-whipped. Cole relied on his years of field experience to smooth out the smile tugging at the corners of his mouth. He began mentally adjusting his profile of the forty-something tennis-playing socialite. Traxton wasn't the most macho of men, but then neither was Donald Trump. Still, with his money, he could get all the women he wanted.

For him to sign up for marriage this late in the game, the future Mrs. Traxton must toss some major ass in the bedroom.

Mildly curious, Cole asked, "When do I meet her?"

Traxton raised his right arm and gave a quick glance to the Rolex on his wrist. "Alex should be back from lunch now." Leaning over his desk blotter, he punched the intercom button on his phone. "Fiona, buzz Miss Kendall and tell her we're ready for her."

Alex! Miss Kendall!

Cole's heart slammed into his chest, a montage of memories firing off in his head. Alex, warm brown eyes damp with laughter, rolling onto her side and warning him to stop tickling her before she peed on his quilt. Alex, the lover who came so hard the last time they were together she trembled from head to toe for a full five minutes. Alex, the woman he couldn't seem to burn out of his brain no matter how many late nights and crack-of-dawn mornings he logged in.

Fingers digging into his wrist, Cole turned to the door. Overwork must be making him sloppy because while he'd gone over the company roster of key executive and managerial staff, he hadn't bothered to check its R&D department, reasoning that lab rats pretty much stayed put…well, in the lab. Projecting scenario outcomes was among his special skill sets; but in a million years he couldn't have guessed a routine client interview would turn out like this.

Any minute now he would be face-to-face with Alex. Adrenaline ripped through him, electrifying his muscles and his mind. The rush it brought felt like being back in the field with the bad guy finally framed within his rifle crosshairs, only in this case the waiting hadn't gone on for days or even weeks but years.

Over the blood roaring inside his ears, he heard the office

door opening. A pair of long, slender, silk-sheathed legs cleared the threshold. He remembered those legs wrapping around his waist while he lost himself inside her, and an invisible fist plowed into his gut.

Alex froze, one beige platform pump planted inside the threshold, the other still out in the hall. Like a fashion mannequin posed in mid-stride, she looked entirely too perfect to be real, her stalled smile so stiff it might have been painted on, her stunned gaze dead as a doll's. Gone were the wind-whipped curls he'd used to love running his fingers through. She wore her hair poker-straight and pulled back from her temples in a bun so tight he had to believe the corners of her eyes must hurt. Without checking her labels, he surmised her beige silk suit must be Chanel, her shoes Manolos, and her pearl earrings Miki Modo.

Gone were the artsy tops and the faded jeans that rode low on slender white hips, the scuffed cowboy boots and funky jewelry she'd trolled for in secondhand stores, the quirky laugh and lopsided smile and the host of other wonderful, *colorful* traits that had made her Alex to him. Had they been passersby on a crowded Manhattan street, he couldn't say for certain he would have known her. When had she become so tailored, so buttoned down? When in God's name had she started wearing beige?

Traxton crossed to the front of the desk. "Alex, allow me to introduce Cole Whittaker, the private-security guru I spoke about."

Traxton's voice seemed to snap her out of her trance. She entered the rest of the way and drew the door closed.

She turned toward Cole, a faint flush limning her high cheekbones. "Mr....Whittaker?" Both a pause and a question mark punctuated the address, but then five years ago, she'd known him as Cole Calhoun. She crossed the carpet toward him, beige like nearly everything else in the room, and stuck out her hand. "Randall's been gushing about your firm for days now."

He'd been wondering how she was going to play it and now he knew. Fortunately he'd been keeping secrets for most of his life.

He unclenched his hands and reached around with his right. "Ms. Kendall."

His hand closed over her slender one, the fingers cold as snow, the once-bitten-to-the-quick nails grown out to medium length and sporting a French manicure. A flash of fire drew his attention to her left hand. Set in thick platinum, the canary diamond occupied most of the real estate on her ring finger.

He let her hand slide away and stepped back. "Your fiancé was just briefing me on your Belize trip."

Traxton stepped up between them. "Mr. Whittaker has expressed some reservations about accepting this assignment. I'd hoped meeting you would convince him."

He slid a proprietary arm around Alex's waist—classic male marking behavior—and Cole couldn't help wanting to rip the limb right off. But Alex wasn't his lady anymore. She was Traxton's, and the rock weighing down her left hand showed she'd granted the CEO the right to touch her.

Traxton's dark head swiveled back to Cole. "Now that you've met Alex, I trust you see why her safety and well-being are so critically important to me?"

Alex looked about as comfortable as a kid called to stand up in front of the dinner company and recite a poem. Reaching down, she moved Traxton's hand aside.

"I don't think Mr....Whittaker should be pressured. If he has reservations or prior commitments, then surely we can come up with someone else."

She stood close enough for Cole to catch a hint of her perfume. The light floral fragrance might as well have been a time-travel machine. It carried him back to sweat-dampened sheets and tickling matches at midnight and showers held off until the last possible moment on Monday mornings so he could keep her with him if only through her scent.

Shaken by the powerful olfactory memory, he anchored his gaze to Traxton. "Guidepost specializes in managing high-risk scenarios. The mission you've briefed so far sounds routine. If you won't accept one of my associates, then I'll be happy to recommend other firms that provide basic bodyguard services. There's no point in paying for a Mercedes when a junker will get the job done just as well."

Traxton and Alex exchanged glances. Alex looked away, but not before Cole caught her raking her teeth over her bottom lip as she used to when she was nervous—or trying to hide something. Wariness crawled up his spine like a spider.

Traxton blew out a heavy breath. "There is the matter of a rather…unpleasant note left for Miss Kendall last week."

Earlier he'd sensed the man was holding information back and the sheepish looks on his and Alex's face confirmed it. Without hearing the rest, Cole already knew they were going to need that Mercedes after all. They were going to need him.

Dividing his gaze between them, he demanded, "How unpleasant?"

Alex spoke up, "I'm sure it's a hoax, nothing more."

"I'll be the judge of that." He turned to face her. "What did this note say exactly?" For a second, he almost slipped and called her Lex.

She hesitated, wetting her lips. "It said if I went to Belize, I'd die."

"What did it say *exactly?*"

She opened her mouth to answer him, but before she could, Traxton interrupted. "We believe it to have been written by someone at Sun Coast, a banal scare tactic to bully us into sending someone less prepared to brief the proposal to the Belizeans. Rivalry is the nature of capitalism, after all."

Cole glared at Traxton. He hadn't liked the CEO before, but he liked him a hell of a lot less now.

"Rivalry, yes. Death threats, no. Why didn't you mention this earlier?"

Traxton had the audacity to shrug. "I'd hoped to have your signature on our corporate consulting agreement first. The nondisclosure clause has been carefully crafted by our legal department. Obviously this…incident is not something I want leaked to the press, especially at such a sensitive time."

"Obviously." Ordinarily a prospective client questioning his professionalism would have sent Cole walking out the door, but with Alex's safety at stake, he let it go—for now. "I want to see that letter, the original, not a copy."

As soon as he left Traxton's office, he would head for the FBI Crime Lab's Manhattan Office. If it meant calling in every favor chip he had out there, the lab boys would go over that letter with the forensic equivalent of a fine-tooth comb. With television shows like *CSI* unwittingly spreading the word about the merits of latex gloves and bleach, the letter would likely come up clean. Still, if there was any DNA trace evidence, he meant to uncover it.

"I assume that means you've decided to accept my offer and staff the project personally?" The gleam in the CEO's gaze and the smug smile pulling at the corners of his mouth told Cole the guy knew what his answer would be.

Out of the corner of his eye, he watched Alex. A part of him hoped she might urge him to say yes, too, but the frozen mask was back in place, her eyes empty. Knowing he was about to give her yet another really good reason to hate him, he said, "There is another alternative. You could send someone in Miss Kendall's place, a man."

Predictably her mouth fell open. "Corporate decisions on project staffing are none of your concern, Mr. Whittaker."

Traxton frowned. "Really, Alex."

Dodging her dagger look, Cole turned to Traxton. "Actually it is very much my concern. In fact, it's my business. Risk-assessment and management are among the key services Guidepost provides. Sometimes the best way to manage risk is to avoid it altogether."

Color high, she turned to Traxton. "It's obvious Mr. Whittaker has strong reservations about accepting this assignment. He's the one who needs to be replaced, not me. He admitted there are other private security companies that provide executive protection."

Hating to hear his own words used against him, Cole spoke up. "There are, but Guidepost is the best. I'm the best." If she was hell-bent on going, he was just as hell-bent on going with her.

Traxton answered with a nod. "Mr. Whittaker's braggadocio is justified. Beyond his firm's very impressive corporate capabilities, his personal reputation as a hostage rescuer, high-speed evasive driver and sniper is without peer."

"Fortunately we're not going to require Mr. Whittaker's expertise because I'm not going to need rescuing. That note is nothing more than a hoax. You said so yourself."

"And so I believe it to be. Still, there's no point in assuming an unnecessary risk."

"But—"

He silenced her with a flick of his hand, a trick Cole had

to admit he'd never managed. "No buts. Remember our agreement."

Standing across from him, Alex seemed to shrink.

"Splendid, then it's settled." Traxton caught Cole's eye. His smug smile seemed to say, *see how easy that was?* "I'll leave word with Fiona to make certain the jet is stocked with beluga and Stolichnaya."

Watching the dynamic unfold, Cole felt a tight ball of anger curl up inside him. Clearly Alex's hairstyle and clothing weren't all that had changed. The woman he'd known and, yes, loved five years ago would have hauled out her dog-eared copy of *The Feminine Mystique* and told Traxton just where he could shove it. Back then she'd also gotten silly on a few sips of cheap Chianti and inhaled ballpark hot dogs as though they were the finest filet. His beat-up Ford pickup had taken them everywhere they wanted or needed to go. There'd been backpacks for pillows, and flannel shirts and jeans and sloppy foods buried beneath ketchup and washed down with beer, not private jets, catwalk couture, caviar and vodka—or empty eyes.

He hauled himself in. His mission was to escort her to Belize and back—period. For him to do his job he needed to start seeing her as his "principal" and not as the woman he'd once deeply loved.

The inter-office buzzer sounded. "Excuse me." Traxton walked over to the desk. "Yes?"

Cole and Alex eyed one another as the secretary's British-accented voice filled the room. "My apologies for the interruption, sir, but you asked me to remind you of your luncheon appointment. Your driver is waiting below."

Traxton's dark head bobbed. "Thank you, Fiona. I'm on my way."

Cole locked his gaze on Alex. "Miss Kendall, is there somewhere we can go to continue our discussion?"

Snapping his briefcase closed, Randall called out from the desk, "Why not stay and use my office? I won't be back for several hours." He picked up the case and rounded the desk.

"That'd be great, thanks."

Alex opened her mouth as if to refuse, but Cole snagged her gaze, willing her to read his mind as she'd used to. *Go ahead, I dare you.*

She straightened her already impeccable posture to stiff-as-board status and snapped up her chin. Her eyes and body language both read, *Bring it on.* Apparently her biddable behavior was limited to interactions with her fiancé. "Yes, thank you, Randall. My office is a mess at the moment."

Her gaze flickered over to Cole. The glimmer in her eyes told him the old Alex wasn't really gone, not entirely.

Randall came up between them, ending their standoff. "I'll talk with you later."

The light in her eyes dimmed, and she lifted her lips into a strained smile. "Have a good lunch."

Alex walked him to the door, her back to Cole. A peck on the cheek sent Randall exiting the office. From a few feet away, he could almost hear her brain ticking like a time bomb, counting down to some already determined number, most likely ten.

At what he figured for nine or near to it, she whipped around. A blind man couldn't have missed the barbs firing from those beautiful honey-drizzled irises.

"What the hell are you doing here?"

3

NOT WAITING for Cole's answer, Alex slammed the office door closed. She marched back across the carpet, feeling her carefully constructed world, her new life, break apart a little more with every retraced step.

"I could ask you the same thing." He punctuated the statement with a shrug.

She glared at him so hard her eyes hurt. His matter-of-fact attitude made her feel worse than if he'd slapped her. Slapping would be honest, at least, but then it seemed he'd never come close to that, certainly not with her.

"*I* work for this company." Needing to put some distance between them, she rounded Randall's desk and slipped behind his high-backed chair.

"For the next week, so do I."

Bracing her hands on the leather back, she struggled to keep her breathing even and her head clear. "Given that I'm supposed to be walking you through the trip agenda, I should probably point out it's four days, not a week."

His mouth parted in the sexy half smile that used to melt her. "I get compensated for travel time to and from Denver."

So he was still in Denver. That was…interesting. Reminding herself she couldn't care less where he lived, or how, or who with, she demanded, "Are you really an FBI agent or are you some kind of con artist, Mr. *Calhoun*?" She said the alias with a deliberate emphasis.

His jaw tightened, a subtlety that most people would have missed, but then she'd known him so well—or so she'd thought. "I *was* an FBI agent, a sniper on the Agency's Hostage Rescue Team. When I met you, I was undercover."

Her nails sank into the soft leather. "So your dream of taking the band on the road, of going to Nashville to cut an album, all that was a lie?"

She didn't bother trying to keep the bitterness from her voice. Over the years, she'd fantasized any number of reunion scenarios, some sexy, some violent; the latter usually took the form of a blistering verbal battle she invariably won. Now that she was living the reality, seeing him again just flat-out hurt.

Expression sober, he nodded. "Believe me, Alex, I didn't like lying to you. I hated it, but that's what being undercover involves. Every member of that band was an agent working the same case. Telling you the truth would have jeopardized not only my cover but theirs, too. Once we met, the only way I could keep seeing you was as Cole Calhoun."

She lifted a hand from her hip. Raking cold fingers through her scalp, too late she remembered she wore her hair pinned in a bun. "I suppose leaving me alone wasn't one of the options you considered?"

"I wasn't looking to meet anyone that night. Meeting someone was the farthest thing from my mind. It just happened, *we* happened, and I kept telling myself that the mission would wrap soon and once it did I'd come clean with you. But instead it dragged on week after week. And then my pager went off when I was on my way to the airport to pick you up. Three hours later I was on stakeout in the mountains, in a high-security lock-down situation, no cell phones allowed."

She shook her head. He wasn't getting off that easy, not after five years. "You had three hours. That's plenty of time to make a call. But instead you left me hanging without a word. Those first few hours standing alone in the airport were hell. I was sure you must be hurt or dead, that there'd been an accident. I called every hospital, every emergency number I could think of. Funny thing, none of them had any Cole Calhouns. When I finally calmed down and called the bar where we met, where you supposedly worked, the manager told me you'd quit. Funny thing, though, you couldn't be bothered to leave a forwarding address so he could mail your paycheck. That's when I knew you weren't coming for me, not that day, not ever." Fair or not, after five years of silence it felt good to let it rip.

He dropped his voice. "When an agent's pager goes off, any choices you might have had thirty seconds before fly right out the goddamned window."

"You had a choice and a cell phone. You could have at least called and told me you had to cancel, that something had come up."

"No, I couldn't. And if I had, you wouldn't have settled for that, and we both know it. You would have pressed for an explanation I couldn't begin to give."

"Pu-leeze, spare me the would-haves, should-haves, could-haves. You had an easy relationship out and you took it, end of story." And it was the end of the story, theirs at least.

His brows snapped together. "Choice is a two-way street. You were the one who chose not to return my calls, to block my e-mail address, to set that dragon of a mother of yours on me—"

"What did you expect? That I'd welcome you with open arms when you finally decided to get back in touch six weeks later? And now five years after the fact you decide to turn up in New York in time to go to Belize with me!"

"I didn't 'decide to turn up.' Your fiancé flew me out here. Look, until you walked into this office, I had no idea you were my principal." He blew out a breath and admitted, "I didn't even know you were in New York."

Alex released the chair back. The rage that had ripped through her was ebbing, which was just as well. A full-scale shout-out might feel good for the moment, but like all passionate releases, in the end there was always a hefty price to pay.

"Under the…circumstances, don't you think you should… I don't know, recuse yourself or something?"

He shook his head. "I'm the best, Alex, or at least there's nobody who does what I do better than I do. I'll keep you safe, get you to Belize and back, and then I'll walk out of your life for good this time…if that's what you still want."

If that's what you still want. "Of course it is," she snapped. "I'm getting married, remember?"

His blue eyes froze to ice chips. "Congratulations. I hope Traxton realizes what a lucky man he is." It was just the sort of empty compliment she'd expect from a seasoned player.

"As soon as I close this deal with the Belizean government, I can focus on the wedding. Neither of us wants a big church thing, just a dash into City Hall and then brunch at the Ritz." She stopped when she realized she was probably overdoing it.

He folded his arms over his chest. "Sounds like you've got things all figured out."

She heard the irony in his voice but chose to ignore it. "I guess I do." *Breathe, Alex, just breathe.* "Four days including travel, and then you're out of here and gone from my life, got it?"

"Got it. For now, you're supposed to be briefing me on the trip. That wasn't just bullshit I put out there for Boyfriend's benefit. I'll expect an itinerary first thing tomorrow morning, though by C.O.B. today would be better."

She clenched her hands on her hips. "Look, Whittaker, you're a contract employee, a temporary hire. You don't get to make demands."

One dark brow lifted. "I wouldn't be so sure about that. Remember, *Miss Kendall,* without me you don't get to go to Belize."

THAT NIGHT Cole sat in the airport bar, cell phone pressed to his ear while he waited for his flight to come in. There was no point in staying the night, and once he got back to Denver he'd have to haul ass to get everything done to tie up loose ends on other projects before he headed back to New York next week.

He figured he might as well use the downtime to get Les on the line and tell him what under other circumstances would have been incredible news.

"I closed the Traxton Biotech deal a couple of hours ago. He's ponying up triple our trip fee plus expenses."

"That's great news, but it almost sounds too good to believe. What's the catch?"

Cole hedged. "No catch. You know the type. Has more money than he knows what to do with and likes to wave it around. In this case, he wants a bodyguard to escort his Director of R&D to Belize and back for a presentation—standard stuff."

"Sounds like a paid vacation if not free money. Should I be jealous?"

No, definitely not. "I was in Belize before—back when I was still on the team. It's hot, humid and still definitely Developing World. Believe me, I'll be envying you back in Denver."

"Yeah, well..." Les hesitated. "Is everything okay?"

Cole paused in peeling the label off his half-finished beer. "Sure, why wouldn't it be? I'm a little jetlagged, but otherwise..."

"You sure that's all?"

"Yes, Mommy, I'm sure."

Les laughed. "Okay, okay, point taken. Have a good flight."

Clicking off Cole looked across the bar to the bottles ranged along the mirrored wall and for the first time in years considered trading in his beer for something stronger—say, a Scotch. Other than the very occasional cocktail, he hadn't drunk hard liquor since he'd left the Agency a couple of years ago. In the unlikely event that he lived to grow old, he'd carry every damnable detail of that past day on the job with him to the grave.

The gang known as the Spiders had been shaking down local merchants for a decade. In addition to the petty theft and random bullying, there was a nasty racial component to the targeted violence. The call that day involved a convenience store holdup on Colfax Avenue. Ordinarily, local police would be the responders, but in this case the perpetrators were gang members linked to several bank robberies as well. Their latest day's work had left the sixty-something convenience-store owner not only with an empty till but also a broken nose and a bloodied eye that would likely require surgery to save. As a final straw, just to show what bad asses they were, they'd put a bullet through his dog.

Maybe it had something to do with his "Pop-Pop," his mother's father, owning a convenience store where as a kid Cole had loved hanging out, or maybe he'd watched way too many Lassie reruns growing up. More than likely it had to do with having just left his hundred-and-twenty-fifth unreturned message on Alex's voice mail, which he'd sworn would be his last. For whatever reason, Cole was operating on a shorter fuse than usual, and the punk, all of sixteen, must have sensed it.

Hand on his holster, Cole called out for the kid to drop his weapon. That was usually the point where they tossed whatever they had as far as they could and ran like hell.

Only this kid held his ground, turned around and waved the gun in the air. Grinning like a clown, he called out, "Come and get me, G-man."

And Cole had. Without calling for back-up, he'd pulled his pistol from the holster, slid off the safety and pulled back on the trigger. The .22-caliber bullet whizzed past the kid's left ear exactly where he'd aimed, near enough to give him a good scare but with enough clearance to make sure it didn't come into contact with actual flesh and bone. Eyes wide, the kid dropped the gun and fell to his knees in one smooth, almost choreographed motion. Cole made the collar, no sweat—and lost his career.

His first action after turning in his badge was to buy a bottle—several bottles. He picked up a half-dozen fifths of Glenlivet and a bag of potato chips. Other than the chips, which he finished off in the first hour, and the bag of moldy white bread on his kitchen counter, he didn't eat for the next five or so days. He spent what was left of that week and most of the next drunk, dangerously drunk, drunker than he'd ever been or imagined being, drunker than any sane person who gave a shit about himself would ever become. What he experienced wasn't a spiraling downward so much as a fitful floating. Mostly he'd drifted, drifted between coming to enough to drink some more and sprawling flat on his back unconscious. That alcohol poisoning hadn't killed him made him seriously rethink his mother's belief in guardian angels. If a member of the heavenly host had been riding shotgun at his couch-side, it must have been woozy from the fumes.

Afterward, there weren't pieces to pick up so much as cinders to sift. He'd uncovered the concept for Guidepost buried deep beneath the rubble. Basically, it was a compromise, a way to do the work he loved, still, only in a private-sector playing field where bucking protocol wasn't always a deal buster. Sometimes it was a real plus.

Five years later, he'd just gotten to the point where he felt comfortable in his life. And then on a routine client interview on a day like any other, Alex Kendall had walked—literally—back into his life, and anything close to comfort had shot straight to hell.

He held up a finger to the bartender, signaling for another beer.

ARMS FULL, Alex stormed into her Union Square apartment later that evening, certain smoke must be spouting from her ears. It really sucked when the person you were most furious with was yourself. Why, oh, why, had she chickened out on telling Randall about her past with Cole?

Because she wanted to go to Belize, that's why, and for whatever reason, he obviously had his heart set on Cole escorting her there. Okay, maybe there was more to it than that—her ex's ice-blue eyes raking her over could be pretty unnerving—but for right now she was sticking to her story. It was all about business, being practical, getting the job done.

Yeah, right, Alex, her inner voice, crowed. *You used to write fiction but apparently now you just live it.* Though she'd given up writing, like a woman scorned, her muse had never entirely exited the scene.

Stepping into the kitchen, she flung the grocery bags containing cat food, paper towels, assorted single-serving frozen dinners and dental floss down on the granite countertop along with her keys. An open bottle of shiraz sat out on the counter. She grabbed a lipstick-stained wineglass from the sink, half-filled it, and knocked back a long, soothing swallow.

Her feline "children," Tessa and her daughter China Blue aka Boo-Boo, trotted up to her. The tiger-striped tabbies stropped her ankles and meowed, Tessa's vocalization almost an operetta, China's a pseudo squeal. Both cats looked up at her with wide, expectant eyes. Clearly this wasn't just a social call.

She squatted down, reaching out to scratch two lifted chins. "Hey, girls, miss Mommy? Silly question, of course you did. It's dinnertime, and you two may have the brains and beauty in the family, but I, my loves, have the opposable thumbs."

Standing, she popped the lids on two cans of Fancy Feast—they still refused to touch the grayish, supposedly all-natural stuff—filled the houndstooth-print ceramic bowls, and set them down. The moment the bowls touched the floor, the cats dropped their heads and tucked in. Lapping sounds filled the narrow kitchen. Alex let out a sigh, picked up her wine and slipped off her shoes. On the surface, it was an evening like any other, and yet she couldn't shake the feeling the walls of her rebuilt world were once again on the verge of tumbling down because of one man. Cole Calhoun. On second thought, she'd better get used to thinking of him as Cole Whittaker.

Coming face-to-face with him after all this time was the equivalent of an emotional body slam. She hadn't felt so panicked since she'd fallen down the stairs on her sixth birthday and it had taken several seconds, which had felt like hours, for her to breathe again.

His airport no-show five years ago had knocked the wind out of her sails for a good long time. When no amount of Ben and Jerry's or cheap sangria could budge him from her brain, she'd turned to sex. There'd been a crazy self-destructive six months when she'd gone through lovers like tissues during cold-and-flu season. But just as she couldn't eat or drink away the hurt, sex hadn't worked any better. No lover could come close to matching Cole in bed or out, and to be fair, she'd been too emotionally shut down, too numb to be much of a sexual partner in return. In the end, she'd given up her apartment and moved back in with her parents. For three months, she'd lain in her childhood bed and listened to the bathroom faucet drip while she tried to figure out where to go with her life.

Writing down her pain was the one thing that saved her. Admittedly her novel of an idealistic young biologist who travels to Denver and finds unexpected and apparently unrequited love was more autobiography than fiction. Then again, every English teacher she'd ever had advised "write what you know." Her "raw honesty" and "stunningly spare prose" had won her reviews ranging from raves to respectable, but sales had still tanked. Thank God she had her science degrees to fall back on, a bachelor's in biology and a master's in microbiology. She landed a job as a tester at Traxton's offsite lab in New Jersey. Even though it was a dead-end job, she'd worked her ass off, not because she was dedicated but because staying late meant spending less time alone in her apartment.

Eight months into the job, she came face-to-face with Traxton. It hadn't been a planned thing. Wearing a lab coat, shower-wet hair and no makeup, she hadn't set out to catch anyone's eye. Still, he'd invited her to the head office in Manhattan to talk about her career future. In the course of the day, which included a private tour of the facility, a five-course lunch in the executive dining room and drinks back in his private conference room, it became clear his interest in her went beyond the professional. She was moderately attracted to him but mainly she was flattered. Still, dating your boss was almost always career suicide. She turned down his dinner invitation flat.

But whatever else Randall was, he was determined. Her

refusal only fueled his persistence. When after six months he still hadn't lost interest, she'd given in. Drinks at St. Regis's King Cole Bar, followed by dinner at Sardi's and then back to his penthouse on the upper west side for cognacs and, of course, sex. The chemistry between them wasn't incredible, at least not on her side, but there was enough interest to keep the sex satisfying. For a man pushing fifty he had impressive stamina. She suspected he might owe the latter to some pharmaceutical help, though the only pill she'd ever seen him swallow was a men's multivitamin. Theirs wasn't a fairy-tale relationship by any means, but it worked, they worked, and she had to believe once they settled into married life they'd make a solid team.

And now Cole had barged back into her life, causing her to question it all.

She'd been completely clueless when she'd stepped inside Randall's office, a walking target, a sitting duck. Not in a ga-zillion years had she considered that the private security firm her fiancé insisted on hiring was owned and operated by Cole!

But back when they'd met he'd been an FBI sniper, a glo-rified government assassin. She was still working to wrap her brain around that. Even if the people he'd shot down were the bad guys, it must take a certain personality type to stalk someone for weeks, maybe months, watch them sleep and eat, make dinner and make love, and then one day pull back on the trigger and end their life. At least that's how she imagined it must go down. Someone who could do that for a decade and still sleep nights must be a different breed of biped.

Five years ago they'd just about burned up the sheets. Sex like that made a person lose touch. She'd been so sure she was in love with him—that he was The One—she'd never stopped to ask the hard questions—or many questions at all. How did a country singer swing the rent on a loft apartment in one of the trendiest districts in downtown Denver? Why couldn't he ever take a few days off and come to Philly to see her for a change? Were they in a relationship or at least moving toward one or just hanging out? All that time, Cole "Calhoun" had never really existed.

As far as appearances, he hadn't changed much—a little older but mostly leaner, harder. His wavy hair was as thick as before but with more salt than pepper. The silver suited him. So did the lines etched into his forehead and creasing the corners of his blue eyes, eyes that still seemed to see straight through her. His bullshit barometer, he'd used to call that long, steady stare.

And suddenly she was remembering other things, too, not whole scenes but snippets, highlights, as though that month five years ago was a movie trailer, her very own evening at the Oscars. The weight and taste and texture of him gently stroking inside her mouth, the lost look washing over his face just before he came, the slow, thorough way he made love to her on Sunday mornings before they had to get up for him to drive her to the airport. Kneeling between her splayed thighs, he used to sit back on his heels and spread her wide with his fingers and savor her with all his senses, starting with his eyes. He'd made her feel things she'd never imagined she could feel, never known even existed outside of romance novels and chick flicks. And the whole time he'd been playing her, lying to her about who he was right down to his name.

She stared at the phone and briefly considered calling Randall and spilling her guts after all. It wasn't too late. Once she explained that she and Cole had a prior relationship, surely he would agree to hire another security company. But no, talk about self-defeating. Randall might not be the hard-nosed bastard in his personal life that he was in business, but she didn't kid herself that he would respond with selfless understanding and complete nobility, either. He had a man's ego, which was to say super-sized. Once the information sank in, he would strike out, and not just by firing Cole. At minimum, he would make her answer questions—lots and lots of questions. The prospect of being interrogated by her fiancé on the topic of her former lover suddenly seemed altogether horrific.

Maybe the worst was over. Other than the time she and Cole would be trapped together on the plane, she shouldn't have to see him all that much. As she understood the job, a bodyguard was supposed to stay behind the scenes. With luck, she'd be so busy schmoozing government officials and prepping for her presentation that she'd forget he was even there.

And when circumstances called for them to interact, she'd force herself to remember exactly how it had felt to stand in the Denver Airport with a backpack of lingerie strapped to her shoulders—and her slashed and broken heart bleeding down her sleeve.

Compared to that experience, Belize would be a cakewalk.

IT WAS LATE that evening when Beethoven finally broke free to make the all-important call. Pacing the carpet's four corners, he had a vision of himself as the lion in the den at the Central Park Zoo—admired but confined, free to move about but only within the gilded domain he'd claimed for himself.

Being extraordinary wasn't always a good feeling.

He picked up his phone and punched in the requisite numbers, knowing that when his associate answered, his restricted number wouldn't show up on any caller-ID machine.

The pickup came just after the third ring, the gravelly voice with its distinctive Brooklyn accent abrupt to the point of rudeness. "Yeah?"

"Alex Kendall left the office an hour ago. The Belize trip is a green light. Cole Whittaker of Guidepost International has been assigned as her bodyguard for the trip."

"Whittaker?" His associate's tone struck him as just a tad too alert, too interested, but he filed that observation away for later recall.

"They leave next Tuesday on the corporate jet. Since you're flying commercial, you'll have to arrive first. I've sent a copy of the travel agenda and e-ticket to your BlackBerry—"

"Got it."

Beethoven ground his teeth. He hated to be interrupted, really he did. "In the meantime, I expect you to find out everything there is to know about Cole Whittaker—what he eats for breakfast, whether he wears boxers or briefs, who, if anyone, he has waiting for him back in Denver."

"Not a problem." A chuckle sounded on the other line. "Expecting skeletons?"

Beethoven hesitated. In the end, he decided against replying. Sometimes the best answer was none at all.

"Just do your job, and you'll be rewarded accordingly." He clicked off on the call.

He was after soft spots, weaknesses, probable points of entry. But skeletons…God, he hoped so. He truly hoped so.

4

One Week Later
Tuesday, Day 1

IT WAS COMING on noon when Cole arrived at the Westches-
ter County Airport thirty-five miles northeast of the city. The
Cessna Citation 10 stood at the ready, the stairs lowered, the
red carpet rolled out over the runway. Traxton's chauffeur
drove across the tarmac and drew up smack beside the plane.
Talk about curb-to-curb.

He climbed out of the car, collected his luggage from the
limo trunk, and walked up the lit steps to the jet. The three-
person crew—pilot-in-command, second-in-command and
flight hostess—greeted him outside the cockpit door. With
their broad smiles, perfectly placed hair and maroon uniforms
they looked altogether too chipper and crisply turned out for
the early hour.

"Welcome aboard, Mr. Whittaker." The SIC reached out to
take Cole's luggage. "Ms. Kendall hasn't arrived yet, but I'm
sure she'll be here shortly."

"I'm sure she will. Thanks."

Cole surrendered his suitcase and followed the pretty,
perky blonde down the maroon-carpeted aisle, the Traxton
Biotech logo, TBT, an intricately woven monogram smack in

the center. The jet seated eight, two rows of side-by-side club-style chairs set on either side of the carpeted aisle. The cabin was a stand-up, which meant he wouldn't be walking like Quasimodo by the end of the almost five-hour flight. The whole damned plane smelled like a shoe department—leather-covered walls, leather-topped banquettes and bar, leather-upholstered chairs. For all Cole knew, the lavatory seat was covered in leather, too.

The twenty-something hostess waited until he'd settled into the plush chair and then launched forward with her spiel. "My name is Kim. I'll be taking care of you today. Once we're in the air, we'll be serving brunch from Zabar's. In the meantime may I bring you a beverage while you wait?" Her china-blue eyes, buried beneath a heavy coating of like-colored eye shadow, flickered over his face.

"Sure, what do you have?" He didn't really want anything, but he sensed he'd have to order something to get her to go away.

As she ran down the extensive roster of refreshments, Cole realized his mistake. Since seeing Alex the week before, he hadn't slept much and the temptation to interrupt and order a big cup of Go the Hell Away was almost too much to resist. He did, though, forcing himself to listen with a patience he didn't feel. Where the hell was Alex?

According to Kim, the five kinds of juices were fresh squeezed and the coffee selections slow-roasted. There was also the ubiquitous fully-stocked bar, including a pitcher of mimosas and another of Bloody Marys at the ready. He'd already had his coffee back at the hotel and drinking on the job was verboten, so he settled on a club soda.

She returned a minute later with a frosted glass and a bottle of Perrier dressed with a lime wedge. He pulled out his snack tray and poured the fizzy designer water into the glass. From everything he'd so far seen he should have figured Traxton wouldn't stock something as pedestrian as generic club soda. What the hell did Alex see in a stuffed shirt like that—well, beyond his bucketloads of billions, that is?

He reminded himself that her personal life was none of his business. That was probably—definitely—for the best. He'd spent the past five years in love with a memory. Who knew, maybe Fate in the form of Randall Traxton had done him a favor. People changed. Alex obviously had. If he was lucky, he might just find he wasn't in love with her anymore. If the other day in Traxton's office was any indication, she wasn't exactly crazy about him.

Still, the thought of anyone threatening her, let alone coming after her, made him certifiably nuts. Even if the author of that threatening letter was just some techno-nerd out for his jollies, Cole was taking the message, the warning, very seriously.

He wished Traxton had. Findings from the lab analysis of the threatening note revealed a mother lode of DNA leavings. There must be trace evidence from everyone employed by Traxton's headquarters office including the CEO.

He pulled out his BlackBerry, checking for messages. Messages, who was he kidding? He was checking to see if Alex had called or sent a text. Other than her assistant e-mailing him the required information, she'd gone radio-silent for the past week. No doubt she was stuck in traffic but on her way.

He put the BlackBerry away and tried relaxing in his seat. The plane wasn't leaving without her. She'd had her secretary pass on her refusal to let him swing by and pick her up, insisting his assignment didn't officially start until take-off. He could have pressed the issue, but there wasn't much point. So long as she was on American soil, she was safe.

Movement at the front of the plane announced she'd arrived.

Hating how his heart kicked into hyper-drive, he pulled out the trip agenda and pretended to study it. One ear cocked, he heard her address the pilots as Bob and Jerry. Being on a first-name basis with the flight crew meant she must come aboard a lot. He wondered how many of those trips had involved pleasure versus business and felt his stomach tighten.

The soft click of heels heading his way had him holding back his breath. Her throat clearing had him looking up. "I don't suppose you could shift over and let me have the aisle?"

"No problem." He slid back his tray, put away his papers and got up.

He'd only left her the window seat to be polite. In a cabin this spacious, you didn't need access to the aisle to stretch your legs. Each club chair was like a mini-recliner with plenty of room between seats.

The next few minutes were spent making the switch. He tried not to notice how good she smelled and looked. Today's ensemble was a white silk collared blouse and a pale yellow linen suit, not beige but close enough. She bent to slide her laptop case beneath the footrest, treating him to a bird's eye view of her behind. Her ass looked just as firm and delectably packaged as he remembered, the brief glimpse of panty line showing she was wearing a thong. Apparently not everything had changed.

She slipped into the seat and pulled out the tray. "Thanks. The sunlight bleeds out my screen." She lifted the computer case onto the tray and unzipped the side. Their late take-off was to accommodate Alex's morning meeting, namely the all-important hand-off of her other projects to her assistant. And yet here she was, apparently still on the J.O.B.

"You and that thing don't part company much, but then I guess time is money." He hadn't really meant to start off the trip being an asshole. But seeing her made his mouth go off like a runaway train.

"Yes, it is." She reached for her safety belt. "By the way, I think it's best if we keep things strictly professional over the next four days."

He stiffened. Did she think he planned on hopping her bones? Not that he'd mind doing so, but the implication that he couldn't control himself rankled. "Fine by me, I wouldn't have it any other way."

"Good, we're on the same page then, Mr. Whittaker." Gaze glacial, she fastened the seat-belt buckle with a snap.

"Mr. Whittaker?"

She turned her head to look at him. "I'd prefer no first names, assuming Cole is even your real name—or was that a lie, too?"

So much for letting bygones be bygones. "It's my real name all right. So is Calhoun. It's my middle name and my mother's maiden name."

She rolled her eyes as if to indicate just how not fascinating she found all that to be and pulled out a folder filled with computer print-outs.

Now that he'd pushed the envelope, he might as well tear it open the rest of the way. "Speaking of names, once you and Boyfriend tie the knot, are you planning to hyphenate? Kendall-Traxton, that's some mouthful. Your kids will have a swell time filling out college applications."

"Not that it's any of your business, but I'll be changing my name."

"Well, that's not very feminist of you, but whatever floats your boat. I'm sure little Buffy and Randall Junior will appreciate you two keeping things simple."

Her smile thinned. "I think this is the point in our conversation where one of us changes the topic to the weather."

Now that she'd gotten him all fired up, he meant to see this…*thing* through. "Not in my world."

Her gaze shuttered. "You're in my world now."

Other than a slight tightening of her jaw, her expression remained blank, a perfect game face. The Alex he remembered didn't even have a game face. Five years ago he'd been able to read her inside and out, in bed and out of it. He knew the exact spot where teasing her with his fingers and tongue was guaranteed to drive her crazy, the little sounds she made deep in her throat that signaled she was closing in on her climax, the tenderness on her face afterward when he held her close and she melted against him. In ways large and small the woman sitting board-stiff beside him and doing her level best to make sure their shoulders didn't so much as brush was a stranger.

Cole shrugged. "Have it your way…Miss Kendall. Or are you one of those feminists who insist on being addressed as Ms?" The latter he'd added purely to jerk her chain.

He liked her better when she was pissed off. Anger put some color in her Manhattan-pale cheeks, sparked some life into her stone-dead eyes.

The scowl dawning over her features didn't disappoint. "You are positively simian."

He started to point out that once she'd more than enjoyed bringing out the beast in him, but before he could, the plane started taxiing toward take-off and the flight attendant returned to run through the safety procedures.

Alex slanted her gaze away to look out the window, though there was nothing to see but the same gray drizzle making a black ink stain of the tarmac. Her right index finger, restless in her lap, traced invisible circles on her skirt—a textbook sign of evasion. People who dodged seemingly standard questions usually did so with good reason. They didn't want to be unmasked, found out. Staring at her stony profile, he felt a rush of guilt. Whatever had happened to her, was it really all his fault?

What are you working so hard to hide from me, Lex? That you're unhappy? That all this glitz isn't cutting it? That you want—need—something more, something real? That after all this time, you still want...me?

He still had the hots for her, that was a no-brainer, but what he was feeling didn't stop at lust. Lust couldn't begin to explain how he could feel so pissed off at her one minute and so completely tender the next.

Switching gears, he asked, "You ever finish that novel you were working on?"

She kept her gaze fixed out the window, though he sensed her stiffen. "Why do you ask?"

Resisting the urge to reach out and rub the spot between her shoulder blades, he answered, "No particular reason. Just curious." The truth was he'd been rooting for her all these years.

"Yes, I finished it."

"That's good, real good."

She pulled her gaze away from the window and flopped back against the seat. "The reviews were stellar, the sales less so." She stared down at her hands, spread out her fingers. He'd bet anything she was wishing she could take a bite out of one of those gorgeously manicured nails. "It tanked."

"I'm sorry." And he was. Working years to achieve your dream only to have it shot down was tough stuff. He figured he knew how she felt.

She rolled her shoulders, which did interesting things to the front of her silk blouse. "Don't be. It's all worked out for the best."

"At least you finished it. Better than finished, you got it

published. Think of all the people who say they're going to write a book 'someday' but never do."

She angled her face to look at him and rolled her eyes. "Do I look like I need a cheerleader?"

Jesus, he was only trying to be nice. "Maybe this is a good time to go over logistics."

"Logistics?"

He nodded and pulled out the site plan for the resort in Belmopan where they were staying and unfurled it over both their tray tables. He'd drawn up similar diagrams for the U.S. Embassy, the site for that night's welcome reception, and the Belizean ministry's main building, where on Day Two the presentations would take place.

"A bank of elevators goes up from the lobby here." He slid his index finger along the twin boxes representing the elevators. "We have the suite on the second floor. There's an adjoining door leading into a shared living room and kitchenette."

She frowned. "We don't need a suite. Once we get to the hotel, I'll have the clerk switch us to two regular rooms. Better yet, I'll text Terri, my assistant, and have her call ahead and make the change. She must have misunderstood me when I had her book the reservation." She picked up her BlackBerry and started working it with her thumbs as though the matter was settled.

It wasn't. Feeling his tolerance level begin to dip, Cole said, "There's no misunderstanding. I had Terri change the reservation. A suite gives me better access and control, allows me to contain the environment if need be."

Her expression froze, her skin flushed. "Terri reports to me, period. You have no right giving her orders behind my back. While we're on the topic, you have no right interfering with my job in any way."

That did it! Cole stabbed a finger into the space between

them. "You and I had better get something straight here and now. You *are* my job for the next four days. If you so much as fall down and get a bruise on your butt, my ass is on the line for it. I'll be damned if I'll let your feminist pride or your little-girl tantrums or whatever bug has crawled up your butt jeopardize my professional reputation or my firm's. If you have a problem with any of that, say the word now. I'll phone Boyfriend and he can have the pilot turn back. And I'm pretty sure you know what that means. If I don't go, you don't go."

Her eyes widened, her jaw dropped. "You wouldn't dare."

Cole snorted. "Try me."

Seething silence met his challenge. He had her exactly where he wanted her, for the moment at least, and they both knew it.

"Okay, you win—for now." She folded her arms over her breasts—classic protective posture—and glared. "You do your job, and I'll do mine. You can start by waking me up when we're a half hour from landing. I'll need the time to prep. For now what I mainly need is a nap."

He opened his mouth to say he was her bodyguard, not her lackey. Before he could, she'd grabbed her pillow, twisted in the seat, and turned her back on him.

Denver, 2003

"DON'T LOOK NOW but he's coming our way." Jaime's voice was a high whisper in Alex's ear.

Heart pounding, Alex slowly turned in her chair. Her friend hadn't lied. The "he" in question, the cowboy band leader earlier introduced as Cole Calhoun, cut through the women crowding the stage during the set break and headed down the stage steps toward her table.

Breathe, Alex, just breathe.

He reached their table, coming to stand at Alex's chair. Dagger looks shot her way from the disappointed women standing stage-side, but she was too caught up in calming her breathing to care.

"I see you pretty ladies are celebrating a birthday tonight." He tipped his hat to Jaime and Brenda, but there was no mistaking how his ice-blue eyes zeroed in on Alex. "Happy twenty-first, darlin'."

As pickup lines went, you couldn't get much more cornball, but in this guy's case it was all about the delivery. With his lazy-lidded blue eyes, chiseled features and sexy-as-sin smile, he could toss out stale vaudeville one-liners and slapstick routines and still count on bringing down the house—the female side, anyway.

Self-conscious, Alex reached up to straighten her party-store paper tiara, which had listed to the side. "Nice try, cowboy, but the numbers don't lie."

He rested his forearms on the back of the empty chair and leaned forward. His scent—cologne and soap mixed with just the right amount of male sweat—cut through the cigarette smoke and stale beer and wafted toward her. When he turned his head and locked his gaze on hers, she felt as though they were the only two people in the room.

He took off his Stetson and ran a long-fingered hand through his head of wavy dark hair, the stray silver strands twinkling like stars. "I don't care what that crown of yours says, I'm putting my money on twenty-one. A person's first legal drink is a pretty big deal. Next round's on me. What can I get you, honey? And you ladies as well?" His gaze took in their near-empty mugs.

Jaime and Bren exchanged glances and giggled as though

they were back in college. "Tequila shots," they answered in unison. "Only since its Alex's birthday, she needs to eat the worm."

Jaime's elbow knifing her side reminded Alex of her birthday vow to put aside her shyness. Finding her voice, Alex explained, "We were drinking beer, but my friends are trying to get me to switch to tequila. Won't you join us?"

Smiling broadly, he straightened and dragged the chair out from the table. "Thank you kindly. Don't mind if I do."

By the time he went back on stage for the next set and sang both "Happy Birthday" and "She's a Jolly Good Fellow," Alex's head was spinning from her second shot of Cuervo—and her first real shot at falling headfirst in love.

SITTING BESIDE her former lover for a five-hour flight, Alex hadn't expected to sleep, not really. She'd hoped closing her eyes and blocking out the sight of Cole would give her a reprieve, or at least time to reclaim some of her composure, but no such luck. With her eyes closed, her other senses leapt to life, making her even more attuned to him—the warm press of his shoulder against hers, the soft sounds of his breathing, and the fresh, clean scent of him, which always reminded her of the beach. The last time they'd been this close for this long, she'd been wrapped in a bath towel, still damp from their shared shower.

Opening her eyes, she made a show of stretching her arms and arching her back and patting away yawns as though she'd just woken up refreshed from a long, satisfying nap instead of a fitful fake-out. She hadn't logged in a solid night's sleep since she'd walked into Randall's office and seen Cole standing there. Last night had been the worst. Between checking the alarm to make sure she hadn't overslept and getting up to take inventory of her laptop case for the umpteenth time lest she'd forgotten something, she'd logged more time out of bed than in it. After hours on a plane, the dark circles she'd seen in the bathroom mirror that morning must be raccoon eyes by now. There went her plan to show up in Belize looking chic and self-assured.

She turned slowly back to him, wondering how her hair and makeup had fared, wishing she didn't care. "Are we close?"

"We're closing in on thirty minutes from landing." He answered without bothering to look up from the papers on his tray. "I was just about to wake you as per orders. It's time to go over the agenda."

"Again? That's a little anal, don't you think?"

"Talk about the pot calling the kettle black."

"Okay, shoot—so to speak."

She'd been trying for a joke, but her lame attempt had his face turning ashen. "What's that supposed to mean?"

She back pedaled, wondering why he suddenly seemed so angry. "Nothing…well, I mean, you were a sniper, right?"

"I still am."

She studied him out of the corner of one eye, looking at him in a new light. Since the other day, she'd gone to the Guidepost web site and read his bio and résumé not once but many times. The FBI Medal of Honor topped the laundry list of his accomplishments, but it was by no means his only commendation. The extent of his overseas travel was mind boggling—thirty countries, including terrorist hot zones such as Mogadishu and Darfur.

If she were honest with herself, it wasn't only his career that interested her. She'd hoped to get some sense of what had happened in his personal life these past five years. So far, no clue other than the fact he'd kept Denver as his home base.

She remembered his mom had lived there, and he had a younger brother, the one responsible for the soup-can scar. Then again, those could have been lies, too.

Not for the first time she wondered if he had a serious girl-friend, maybe even a live-in. Hell, for all she knew he had a wife. Just because he didn't wear a wedding band didn't mean he was still single. Not everyone was a late bloomer like she was.

One of life's built-in inequities was that men grew distin-guished while women just grew old. When they'd first met, Cole had been a good-looking guy, borderline handsome. Thanks to the patina five years had put on him, he was heart-stopping. She didn't miss the way the flight hostess, Kim, hovered. The number of times she'd stopped by to see if she could refresh his—their—drinks or bring him—them—a snack was almost annoying. It *was* annoying.

"Clock's ticking, princess." Cole's voice startled her back to the moment, "About that agenda."

"Are you always this anal?" she repeated.

He cocked a brow at her. "I prefer *thorough* but yes. That's why I'm the best at what I do."

"Hmm, modest, too, I see."

One side of his mouth curved upward into the slow, sexy smile she used to love, the smile that had turned her inside out. "What can I say? False modesty isn't modesty at all."

Seeing that smile after all these years had her feeling foolish and unsure, like a little girl playing at dress-up—or in her case, corporate executive. To break the tension—hers—she threw the pillow at him. He dodged it, and the makeshift missile sailed over his shoulder. And suddenly the tension between them burst like a bubble. They both broke out laughing.

Pillow in hand, Kim materialized before them. "Did you want me to take this away, ma'am?"

Ma'am. Alex sagged back in her seat. Amazing how one little word and a matter of a few seconds could carry her from feeling like a kid again to middle-aged—old.

5

TRAXTON'S pilot's buttery-smooth landing on the small airstrip just outside of Belmopan heralded a bumpy ground trip. The temperature on deplaning was 91 degrees Fahrenheit, but the humidity made it feel more like 120, the heavy-hanging air causing Cole to remember why seven years ago he and his HRT teammates had joked about needing gills to breathe here. In this part of the world November was still the rainy season. It wasn't raining yet, and the sun striking down on them made crossing the tarmac feel like a beeline through a bed of hot coals. In her sling-backs with the stupidly high heels and paper-thin soles, Alex's feet must feel on fire, though she'd yet to utter so much as a single complaint.

Standing outside the open-air terminal, their luggage piled at their feet, she shifted her laptop case to the opposite shoulder and shielded her eyes with the shelf of her hand. "There's supposed to be a government car to pick us up." She squinted through the wavy lines of heat toward the gate.

Cole doubted it. The tile-roofed terminal was a barebones affair of mostly closed counters and skeleton staff. A limo driver holding up a placard with Alex's name or that of the company would be hard to miss. If he'd been in charge of planning this mission, he would have had them flown into the main airport in Belize City, just an hour's drive away, where ground transportation was plentiful. They could have kicked back, cranked up the rental car's AC, and arrived in Belmopan relaxed and ready to roll out the evening. As it was, though they were only a few miles away, they'd be lucky to get to the hotel in time for a shower before the evening began. Scratch the shower. They'd be lucky to get there at all.

He glanced back at Alex, visibly wilting, and shook his head. "I wouldn't count on that driver showing. If he was going to, he'd be here by now."

Most of her makeup had melted away, including her lipstick, which she'd eaten off in the first few lip-biting minutes when it became clear that they might well be stranded. The humidity had returned her hair to its natural wavy state. Several damp tendrils clung to her temples and nape. A single milky droplet of perspiration slid down the side of her slender throat. Standing beside her, he could almost taste the tang on his tongue. To add insult to injury, the heat had released the scent of her perfume in full force, ferrying him back to every episode of sweaty, satisfying sex they'd ever had—talk about torture. She'd taken off her linen jacket. The back of her blouse was soaked through, revealing the elegant arch of her spine down to the small of her back; the latter, he knew from memory, was the perfect fit for his palm.

He sucked in a breath, feeling his body temperature ratchet upward. His temperature wasn't the only thing on the rise. He sucked in another mouthful of muggy air and tried corralling his thoughts to cold beverages and cold showers and yes, the cold, hard fact that the coming four days weren't a relationship redo but rather a mission like any other.

"Are you always such a pessimist?" She lowered her hand from her face and stared over at him with squinted eyes and a puckered brow.

"I'm a realist, and by the way, where are your sunglasses?"

She bit her lip again. "I forgot to pack them."

"That's a joke, right?" *Who traveled to the tropics without shades?*

She scowled. "November in Manhattan isn't exactly sunshine city, and besides, I figured I'd be spending most of my time in indoor meetings."

Not for the first time he found himself wondering what the hell had happened to the fun-loving woman who'd worn a party-store tiara and boa for her thirtieth birthday, danced the Macarena no matter that it was hokey, and accepted her friends' challenge to eat the tequila worm.

"You're a real party animal these days." He took off his Ray•Bans and handed the glasses over. "Here, wear these until we can buy you some shades."

She hesitated and for a moment he thought she would refuse. Instead she slipped them on. "Thank you." It wasn't exactly a precision fit but at least the tinting would keep the glare from burning out the backs of her eyes. Holding the glasses in place, she took another look around. "It must be coming up to close of business. Maybe our driver got caught up in rush hour or…something?"

Rush hour! Apparently she hadn't completely given up on a career in fiction. "Rush hour implies traffic, which usually means more than one or two cars on the road. Take a good look around, Alex. You see any traffic? You see any cars, period?"

His seven-year-old memory of Belmopan, the Belizean capital, was of a sleepy suburban planned community of non-descript single-story houses, postage-stamp-sized front lawns, and a ring of connecting sidewalks that led back to the market square. Most of the residents worked for the government or in the handful of motels and restaurants catering to tourists. Anything commercial, and there wasn't much, was within a two-block radius.

She intercepted his thoughts with a huff. "Okay, okay, I get it. Knocking my heels together three times and wishing really, really hard isn't going to get us out of here."

Reaching into her bag, she pulled her cell out and started punching the pre-programmed numbers. Several back-and-forth calls between the Belizean point-of-contact and her assistant in New York confirmed what Cole already knew. There'd been a miscommunication. The driver had mistakenly headed an hour away to the big commercial airport in Belize City.

She clamped the cell closed and turned to him, her expression so crestfallen it was hard not to reach out and hug her. "The reception starts at six. It might be my only chance for a word alone with the Prime Minister. You can bet Sun Coast will seize their opportunity."

"It's not your fault, Alex."

He started to reach for her, but she took a backward step, shaking her head hard. "My fault or not, it just is. I've been working this deal for six months, Cole. Winning the contract means a lot to Traxton, but it means a lot to me, too—personally."

And that was all she needed to say. Forget being an "enlightened male." Cole did what he did best. He swung into action, grabbed their luggage and headed back inside.

Struggling to keep pace beside him, Alex craned her neck and asked, "What are you doing?"

"Putting plan B into play."

Out of the corner of his eye, he saw her brighten. "As long as plan B involves getting us out of here, I'm all for it." The grateful expression washing over her fatigued face sent his heart seesawing.

Inside, the still air was stuffier than outside, so he parked her on a bench out front in the shade of a cluster of palms and headed in. The single car-rental counter had a sign saying Closed and there wasn't a taxi in sight. There was one snack counter offering a variety of fruit juices and sodas, candy bars and prepackaged sandwiches. Cole headed over to it.

Snoring drew his gaze downward to a squat woman slumped on a stool, a half-eaten chocolate bar melting through the fingers of her hand. It took a couple rounds of coughs and one really obnoxious throat clearing to get her to open her eyes.

Cole didn't waste any time. "I need to get to Belmopan."

She shrugged meaty shoulders, sucking chocolate off her knuckles, and looked over at him with disinterested eyes.

"Where is the bus stop?" Fortunately for him, the majority of locals spoke English, otherwise he would have had to use his rusty high school Spanish.

She pointed through one dusty glass window to the sidewalk. "The next bus isn't due for another hour." He briefly explained about being stranded, this time reaching inside his wallet and pulling out a Grant. She snapped to attention in her seat, but then, the exchange rate between the Belizean and U.S. dollar teetered around two to one. His fifty bucks was the equivalent of a hundred in her world.

It turned out that her sister, who apparently worked in the kitchen at back, was trying to sell her car. The promise of a hundred bucks American, this time to the sister, got him the keys to a geriatric Ford Grenada with a broken spring sticking up through the front passenger seat and a badly bent driver's-side door. The clunker looked like it had survived a third world war, but it had a half tank of gas, more than enough to get them to Belmopan—assuming the thing started.

They cut through the kitchen to where the car was parked by the Dumpster out back. He got in, turned the key in the ignition and held his breath. The Ford wheezed to life on the second try. He released his pent-up breath, rolled down the window, and handed over the cash.

He circled back to the terminal and drove up to where he'd left Alex waiting. Elbows propped on her lap and chin resting in her upturned palms, she was the classic picture of dejection. Unfortunately for him, she was also sexy as hell. She'd slipped off her shoes. One fancy sling-back sat on its side in the dust. She had her legs open, too, pretty wide in fact, and she'd pulled her skirt above her knees, no doubt to let in the um…air. She must be pretty damned uncomfortable because she'd gone so far as to unbutton her blouse and tie the ends bikini style beneath her breasts. Cole took in her pushed-up cleavage, flat stomach and smoothly slender legs, one word and one word only coming to mind. *Wow!*

She brightened when she saw him, or rather the car. Jumping up, she shoved her feet back into the heels, grabbed her laptop and hightailed it over.

Eyes alight, she bent and leaned into his rolled-down window, so close the tips of their noses almost touched. "You're a miracle worker! How did you possibly manage—" Sudden coughing cut off the rest of the question.

Drinking in her damned perfume—how the light floral fragrance cut through the thick black engine smoke was a mystery—he leaned across the cracked vinyl seat and pushed open the stuck passenger-side door. "Ordinarily I'd do the gentlemanly thing and come over there, but I don't have much faith in this emergency brake, and trust me, turning the engine off qualifies as a really bad idea."

Still coughing, she shook her head, motioning for him to stay put. "I do trust you." She moved around to the other door and grabbed hold of the broken handle.

She trusted him! After the shit that had gone down five years ago, were he in her place he wasn't sure he would trust him. And yet apparently she did, her shining face wearing the look he remembered from five years ago.

Her sudden "Ouch!" tore in on his happy thoughts and had him all but vaulting out of the seat. She sent him a crooked smile and held up her hand to show off her newly broken thumbnail. "I think biting them may have been more practical, cheaper for sure."

He gritted his teeth as she settled their suitcases... Regardless of the reason, sitting by while she lifted their stuff challenged not only his machismo but more fundamentally his manners.

"I know it's not much, the engine's giving out the death rattle, and forget about AC, but if we don't blow up, it'll probably get us as far as Belmopan. I'll figure out plan C once we're there."

"That's quite a sales job, FBI. Are you sure you're not a pessimist?" Her teasing tone assured him it wasn't a serious question. Seeing her so mussed and relaxed and well...free, he had the crazy urge to lean across the seat and plant a kiss on the soft, creamy expanse of her bared belly.

So much for his mission focus. On sniper assignment, it wasn't uncommon to spend up to twelve hours planted in the same position, your reality reduced to the subject framed within your rifle's crosshairs. When you were on duty, you were *on*—period. There were no bathroom breaks or snack breaks or stretching-your-legs breaks. Mostly you either didn't care or didn't notice. When you were one-hundred-plus-percent focused, twelve hours or twelve minutes felt pretty much the same.

Right now he had about as much control over his brain as a hormone-blitzed teenager. Once he got back to the States, he probably ought to seriously do something about getting himself laid, but for the next four days, he had better pull it together. For a bodyguard, losing focus was potentially a very dangerous thing. Assuming the jerk who'd written that death threat was even remotely serious, Cole needed to be totally ready.

She looked as though she was thinking about reaching across the seat bump and patting him on the back. "Seriously, it's got four wheels and at least a partial front seat, so who's complaining?"

Certainly not her. Once she'd realized the driver was a no-show, she hadn't bitched or cried or flipped out. She hadn't looked to Cole to fix things for her, either. Instead she'd pulled out her cell phone and started working on the problem. They'd both been sweating like moose, but her attitude during the phone calls had been cucumber-cool and unfailingly professional. Once he'd come up with a solution, or at least a Band-Aid, she'd piled into a clunker the equivalent of scrap metal on wheels without one word of complaint. She'd actually *complimented* him, called him a miracle worker. And something told him she wasn't just stroking his ego. She'd meant it.

He drove the Ford out the exit gate, following the signs for the Hummingbird Highway. One of the country's four main thoroughfares, the road was only two lanes and land-mined with speed bumps when a turn off was close. On the bright side, at least it was paved.

Surrounded by scenic beauty on both sides and Alex riding

in the shotgun seat, he felt a little like Harrison Ford's Allie Fox in the eighties film, *Mosquito Coast.* The movie had been filmed in Belize, the plot driven by Fox, a Don Quixote-like inventor obsessed with bringing ice to the jungle. An icehouse in the jungle and Alex back in his life, this time for keeps—the odds were pretty much evenly weighed, which was to say 0-0.

To break the silence, he said, "So tell me what's so special about this new natural resource that someone, presumably but not necessarily Sun Coast, would threaten you personally to scare you off from sealing the deal?"

She didn't answer, only fidgeted in her seat. Gnawing at her bottom lip, she turned away to look out the passenger-side window.

Keeping an eye on the highway, he glanced at her. "I've made a career out of keeping secrets, not just those of individuals or agencies but sometimes whole governments." He wasn't bragging, at least he didn't think he was, only stating the facts. "I can probably handle keeping mum on the details of a corporate contract, but, of course, that's your call."

He didn't give a crap about the contract or the newly discovered natural resource it involved, but it hurt that she didn't trust him. Beyond that, he just really liked hearing the sound of her voice.

"You're right. I'm sorry." It was her second "I'm sorry" since they'd landed. Knowing how stubborn she was, not a new thing, he realized they just might be building to some kind of record.

He focused on the highway again, not because he needed to concentrate on his driving—even at this time of day there were hardly enough cars on the road to constitute traffic, let alone rush hour—but because she was so damned beautiful that looking at her for too long made his heart hurt. Even with grease or dirt or whatever the hell it was all over her face and her fancy clothes sweat-stained well beyond the rescue capabilities of the average dry cleaner, she was appealing on absolutely every level in absolutely every way.

"The Belizeans discovered a new sinkhole just off the barrier reef. Sinkholes formed as limestone cave systems during the last ice age when sea levels were much lower. As the ocean began to rise, the caves flooded and the roofs collapsed. Because water circulation is poor, a sinkhole doesn't support most sea life. What it does support is large numbers of bacteria."

Cole was no scientist, but he knew that in addition to commercial usages as fermenting agents, bacteria had chemical and pharmaceutical applications as well.

Alex turned to face him. "The Belizeans have harvested a new strain of bacteria that if distilled and marketed properly could revolutionize industrial clean-up. *Exxon Valdez* was a testing ground for using bacteria as a biodegradation agent for petroleum contamination, but back in '89, the response efforts were largely trial-and-error. Almost twenty years later, more than 26,000 gallons of oil still contaminate that Alaskan shoreline. Once Traxton wins the sole right to develop the smart bacteria and register the patent, Prince William Sound will be our first large-scale test site. But first we have to win." The light beaming from her eyes had him forgetting to breathe.

She fell back against the sun-faded vinyl. "I'm boring you. I'm sorry. I have a tendency to get a little too passionate, but I really believe in this project."

"I can tell."

Once Cole had been passionate, too, passionate about fighting the good fight and bringing the guys in the black hats to so-called justice, all in the service of the greater good. But that had been a lifetime ago, or so it seemed.

Changing the subject, he asked, "Any ideas on who at Sun Coast might have sent that threatening note?"

Alex hesitated. "Their Director of Business Development, Phillip Collins, isn't someone I've ever considered to have much integrity. He'd be the logical choice, I guess, though a death threat seems pretty over the top even for him. Besides, he's in California. He would have had to arrange for someone local to write and deliver it."

"Any disgruntled employees at Traxton come to mind? Maybe someone on the R&D team who doesn't feel as appreciated as they think they should be?" Out of the corner of his eye, he monitored her reaction.

She hesitated, biting at her bottom lip. "No one comes to mind, but I'll think about it."

"Let me know." The exit for Belmopan was upon them. The turn signal no longer worked so he stuck his arm out the rolled-down window and signaled with his hand. "For now, Cinderella, it's time to haul ass and get ready for the ball."

THOUGH SHE wasn't nearly as well-traveled as Cole, Belmopan didn't resemble any capital city Alex had ever visited. After Hurricane Hattie had almost wiped out coastal Belize City in 1970, moving the capital inland must have seemed the sensible alternative, but the planning committee hadn't factored in aesthetics. A bus station and market formed the heart of the "downtown." They drove a block or so farther, passing a few suburban-style banks, gas stations and restaurants. Just off the market and bus station was Independence Plaza, a campus of granite government buildings that housed the post office and Prime Minister's office. A cross-hatching of sidewalks connected the plaza to the rest of downtown. Unless you were an archeology geek really into Mayan ruins or a nature lover into jungle flora and fauna, there wasn't much doing.

By the time they pulled into their hotel's circular drive, it was coming on 5:15 p.m. local time. Alex grabbed her laptop and rushed inside, leaving Cole to deal with the rest of their luggage. The lobby wasn't air-conditioned but it was noticeably cooler than outside thanks to several ceiling fans and a fountain splashing spray onto the pebbled stucco walls.

Cole joined her at the check-in desk. She didn't have to look over her shoulder to know it was him shadowing her. The heat radiating from him had little to do with the temperature inside or out. And then there was his signature scent, minty soap mixed with spicy cologne.

From behind the desk, a handsome man of late middle age in a crisply pressed linen suit greeted them with a flash of white smile and dark, twinkling eyes. *"Buenos dias, señor, señora.* Welcome to Belmopan, the Garden City." Dividing his gaze between them, he added, "The honeymoon suite, *sí?"*

Alex felt heat blast her cheeks. "We're on a business trip. The reservation is under Traxton Biotechnologies. We're guests of the government."

He glanced down at his reservation book. "Ah, yes, I see it here, a suite with two bedrooms and a shared living space, including a kitchen. Enjoy!"

Now that they'd landed, she figured she had nothing to lose. Avoiding Cole's gaze, she shoved his sunglasses atop her head. "There was a mix-up. The original reservation was for two rooms, two *separate* rooms."

The clerk's smile flattened. "I am sorry…señorita, but that is all we have available. We are unseasonably busy." His gaze wandered over her shoulder to the line forming behind them.

"But I have the confirmation number right here in my

purse." Hands shaking, she tore open her tote in search of her BlackBerry.

Cole stepped up beside her. "We'll take it." Bending to her ear, he hissed, "Nice try, Alex, but if you want to make that welcome reception, I suggest you give it up and get a move on. It's up to you, of course. Me, I get paid either way."

Pride had her opening her mouth to tell him where to shove it, but practicality won out. Two minutes and two keys later, they stood waiting by the mirrored elevators. Staring into the glass, she confirmed she looked as much of a wreck as she felt. Melted mascara had given her raccoon eyes, and the heat and humidity had turned her carefully straightened hair into a wild frizz.

"Where the hell is that elevator?" She stepped forward and punched the up button again, not because she thought it would make things move any faster but mostly because it was something to do.

His gaze met hers in the glass. "Are you always this tightly wound?"

"Sorry. It's just that it took months of prep work and negotiating to get the competition down to just our two firms and so far everything that could go wrong has."

He stepped back from the elevator panel. "That's a little pessimistic, isn't it? For starters, Captain Colgate didn't crash the Cessna. That could have happened, but it didn't. And sure, we missed out on the government wheels, but we got here anyway. And we have a suite that's basically the two rooms you wanted, only we scored a kitchen and a living room, and I'll bet even a partially working TV that gets at least three channels, all of them local. If even one of the two showers pipes up semi-warm water, I'll be in freaking heaven."

She shook her head. "I just want everything to go as smoothly as possible."

"And it's going to." He reached out and laid a hand on her shoulder. Feeling the gentle squeeze of those strong fingers, remembering all the wonderful things they could do, Alex skipped a breath. "Just do us both a favor. Once you get up to our room—*your* room, just kidding—pour yourself a nice glass of minibar wine, take a shower and chill out—or chill out as much as anybody can in almost a hundred-percent humidity."

She nodded, stepping just far enough away that he was compelled to drop his arm. He did and she breathed a sigh of relief.

"You're right. But it'll have to be a short shower. We're closing in on a half hour before we have to leave."

"You could go as you are if you had to. You look gorgeous already."

She shook her head. "It's hot as Hades in here, and even if it weren't, I'd be sweating like a moose from nerves, but thank you anyway."

The corners of Cole's mouth kicked up in his signature sexy smile. "You're welcome anyway." He stepped closer. "Then again, I'm biased. I always did like you sweaty."

The elevator landed with a thump, the double doors dinging open. Alex sucked in a heavy breath and stepped inside. Saved by the bell.

6

MENTALLY kicking himself for that last uncalled for comment, Cole saw Alex safely inside the suite. His only excuse was that it was so damned hot, he couldn't think, couldn't breathe and apparently couldn't resist temptation. Unfortunately, the one appliance that didn't work in the suite was the air conditioning. Other than ceiling fans, they were on their own until he could put in a call for maintenance in the morning. It didn't help his temperature regulation that he could hear Alex stirring on the other side of her room door.

Once he'd showered and poured himself into his tuxedo, there was nothing to do but step out onto the balcony and hope to catch a breeze. He folded his hands behind his back, the right hand cuffing the left wrist, and settled in. He hadn't felt this jittery since he'd picked up his date for his junior prom. Between the girl's Marine dad giving him the third degree and the nosey family rottie they really, *really* should have considered neutering, his nervousness had been justified. He didn't have any such good excuses for himself now.

"It's not so bad out here."

He swung around. The Alex stepping out onto the balcony didn't look like she'd ever touched tie dye in her life. She was so blindingly, breathtakingly beautiful he found it hard to believe he'd ever been lucky enough to be allowed that close.

She'd had the same thirty minutes to get ready that he had. Back in college he'd dated a girl who'd needed that much time just to exfoliate. But here was Alex not only shower-fresh but stunning in smoky eyes and nearly naked lips, upswept hair, and a black linen halter dress that looked as though it was sewn onto her. A seed-pearl choker was her only jewelry unless you counted the rock of an engagement ring, which he deliberately didn't.

In a head-on collision with all that beauty, the only thing he could think to say was, "Wow!"

She dropped her gaze as though embarrassed. "There's a limo on its way to pick us up—*really.* I called," she added, looking up. "It'll be here in about five."

He cleared his throat, which felt as if someone had dumped a shovel-full of sand inside. "Great, here's hoping it has AC. Between you and me, I wasn't sure that clunker was going to make it."

Crazy as it was, he was kind of sorry he wouldn't get to drive her. The drive in had felt…well, almost like they were a couple again.

"I just need to grab my purse."

She turned to go back inside, and Cole sucked in his breath, feeling as though the mugginess had spiked a good ten degrees. Her dress was backless or as close to backless as you could get and still be wearing clothes. The sight of all that creamy, exposed skin had him remembering things he'd rather not right now, like the fact her flesh actually felt every bit as smooth as it looked—and tasted even better. Nope, thoughts like that were definitely not helpful, not unless he wanted to accessorize his tuxedo with a hard-on.

He followed her inside. She darted into her bedroom, the scents of her bath gel and shampoo and perfume lingering in the steamy space.

To distract himself, he asked, "Tell me about tonight."

Through the open door, he heard her rustling. "Okay, what do you want to know?"

"For starters, how do you plan on introducing me?"

She returned to the room with the purse in hand, a beaded black affair not much bigger than a cigarette pack. Opening it, she dropped a lipstick and her room key inside.

Without looking up, she answered, "I hadn't really given it much thought. As my escort, I suppose."

Nice, Lex, really nice. Apparently the new Alex, the one who rode around in private jets noshing on caviar and sporting designer duds, didn't see him as anything more than a flunky.

He focused on keeping his wounded pride under wraps. "As your escort, I'll be expected to have some interaction with our hosts and fellow guests. My advice—if you don't have a plan, or at least a story, then come up with one—fast."

She snapped the purse closed, so hard he was surprised the fragile-looking clasp didn't break, and glared over at him. "Look, this is an important evening for me. Just get me through the front door and then go do your thing and let me do mine. And please, *please,* don't do anything to call attention to yourself."

He held the door for her and stepped back. "I'll hold back from eating the garnishes, if that's what you mean, but as for staying out of your way, I make no promises."

ON HIS previous trip to Belize, Cole had logged most of his stay in the jungle. As he sat in the back of the government limo, it occurred to him that though he'd traveled to thirty countries and five of the seven continents, there were few places he'd ever gone purely for pleasure. Even if he could have found the time, there wasn't anyone he wanted to go with. His business partners were all married with kids. They were lucky to squeeze in an after-hours beer every now and again, forget about going skiing or hiking. He'd never given it much thought before, but suddenly it struck him that he'd spent the past five years pretty lonely.

The limo rolled to a stop, drawing him back to the present and active-duty mode. He looked out the tinted window, getting the lay of the land. The U.S. Embassy was at Embassy Square. Were it not for Old Glory hanging from a flagpole above the entrance, alongside the Belizean banner depicting a shield flanked by two workers in front of a mahogany tree, it would have been indistinguishable from the rest of the granite buildings.

Cole got out and came around to Alex's side. The driver beat him to it, opening her door, and she slid out into the cooling, moist evening air. It was still light outside though the torches had been lit in preparation for the encroaching dusk. Cole looked around, a quick visual sweep of the vicinity meant to search out snipers, suspicious parked vehicles and persons who didn't look as though they belonged. Other than a catering truck parked in a side lot which could present a place for a gunman to hide, the scene looked pretty benign.

He offered her his arm. "Shall we?"

She hesitated and then laid her hand atop his jacket sleeve. Together they walked up the wide limestone stairs to the torch-lit main entrance. Inside the tiled foyer, Alex took the lead, glad-handing their way down the receiving line of distinguished hosts and other guests, including the Belizean prime minister, cabinet ministers and several representatives and senators from Belize's National Assembly, most accompanied by their wives and, Cole surmised, the occasional mistress. With such heavy-hitting guests lining the way, clearing the queue was a time-consuming proposition. Then again, a welcome reception was all about schmoozing.

Chandeliers and sconces lit the main ballroom, where flood lights drew attention to the large mosaic mural celebrating Belizean independence. As guests filtered in, white-jacketed servers circulated the room with trays of champagne flutes and hors d'oeuvres—bite-sized conch fritters, meat-filled empanadas and battered shrimps.

Cole snagged two glasses of champagne and handed one to Alex. She accepted it with a tight smile. "Thanks but I never drink at these things."

Looking into her eyes, he glimpsed a glimmer of the old uncertainty. "Neither do I," he admitted, "so think of it as a prop." He touched his glass to hers. "Break a leg doesn't seem right, so I'll settle for wishing you good luck. You won't need it, though. You're doing great."

He shot her a wink and then turned and headed toward the bar, where he traded in his champagne for a club soda. Big formal parties had never been his thing, and wearing a tuxedo in the heat was pretty torturous, but in the present case both were his job. Drink in hand he circulated the room, blending in with the rest of the penguins. But no matter how many hands he pumped or business cards he took, or sexual passes he dodged from apparently neglected wives, Alex was never out of his sight or rescue range.

The first hour passed slowly. Periodically Alex's voice drifted through the crowd. It was obvious she was a pro at working a room. The Alex he remembered had held on to his arm at parties, shy in large groups. The ease with which she mugged for reporters' cameras and chatted with the American ambassador, Belizean cabinet ministers and other high-profile guests brought home just how far she'd come in five years.

If his pager hadn't gone off that day, if he'd made it to the airport after all to pick her up as planned, would she still have come this far? As much as he wanted to believe so, he doubted it. As always, playing what-if was an exercise in futility. Things had turned out as they had, end of story.

Beyond her new self-confidence, she was breathtakingly beautiful. Who knew a Little Black Dress and pearls could look so amazing? Nor was he the only one to notice how amazing she looked. When they'd first entered the main room, every man sixty and under had done a double-take, every woman had reached for her escort's arm, regarding the "competition" with a tight smile and a wary eye.

As someone who couldn't stop staring at her, Cole couldn't blame them.

Across the room, Alex participated in an animated conversation with the heads of the Belize Chamber of Commerce and Industry, the Belize Business Bureau and the National Trade Union Congress. The three gentlemen showed a tendency all to talk at once, but Alex reined in her tendency to step in and keep order. Her role right now was primarily as an information gatherer, a listener. Brokering a deal of the magnitude of the smart bacteria required keeping the various stakeholders not only informed but feeling as though their voices were heard.

Throughout, she kept an eye on the Belizean Prime Minister, currently in deep conversation with several cabinet ministers. Other than the few words exchanged in greeting on her way inside, she hadn't yet been able to get him alone. Back in the States, she would have worked her way over to join the conversation, but she was in Belize, not New York. The pace was slower here, the vibe much more laid back. Fortunately the night was still young.

Her group was breaking up, so she walked off in search of a glass of water. Halfway to the bar, she caught sight of Phillip Collins, Director of Business Development for Sun Coast, walking her way. She bit back a groan. Running into him tonight was inevitable, but that didn't mean she had to be happy about it. She wasn't.

His usual glass of Scotch in hand, he sauntered over to her. "Alex, you're looking lovely as ever." His thin lips spread into a smarmy smile and he saluted her with his drink. "I hadn't expected to see you here."

"Really, and why is that?"

Try as she might, she couldn't keep the sharpness from her voice. She'd bet money he'd either written that threatening note or, more likely, put one of his minions up to doing it. Either way, he was a scum ball. On second thought, given the way he was eyeballing her boobs, better make that a lecherous scum ball.

"I'd heard there was a mishap with your car."

"Oh, yes, well, it's all straightened out now." She relaxed infinitesimally. Until now she hadn't realized just how much the threatening note had gotten to her.

"Is Randall with you?" He shot a look around the room.

"No, he's in New York. I'm here alone."

She didn't feel alone, though. Ever since she and Cole had arrived and headed for opposite ends of the vast room at her insistence, she'd been deeply, viscerally aware of him, his gaze following her as she moved through the crowd, his big lean body seemingly relaxed but in reality on alert and prepared to pounce into action at seconds' notice. Knowing she was never out of his sight for so much as a minute made her feel both incredibly uncomfortable and incredibly safe, an odd juxtaposition.

He took a step toward her. "In that case, let's call a truce for tonight at least and have a drink together, a real drink."

She backed up. The suffocating feeling of being trapped seized her. He was standing so close she could see the darkish hairs peeking from his nostrils, and she found herself willing Cole to her side.

"I don't think so. I never drink when I'm working, and even if I wasn't, I don't have anything to say to you."

"That's too bad. You're a very alluring woman, Alex. Beauty and the brains to back it up—talk about a winning combination."

He laid a hand on her shoulder. Ordinarily she would knock it off, but she didn't want to make a scene. He was deliberately goading her, she was sure of it. As good as it would feel to slap him or, better yet, wash away his smug smile with the contents of her untouched champagne glass, behaving like an "emotional woman" would be playing into his hands.

"There you are."

Alex swiveled around to see Cole coming up behind her. Relief, gladness and, yes, pride flooded her as he used one broad shoulder to nudge Phillip aside and occupy his place. Standing next to Cole, the other man seemed puny and pale in comparison, but then she expected most men would. Even though Randall was a zealot about both tanning and working out, that day in his office he hadn't fared much better.

Phil divided his gaze between them. Addressing Alex, he asked, "Aren't you going to introduce me to your…?"

She hesitated, briefly considering refusing, but it was a social function. "Phillip Collins, Director of Business Development for Sun Coast Biotech. Cole…Whittaker, the newest member of my…team."

"Welcome to the fun and games of the biotech corporate rat race." Phil turned to Cole and stretched out his hand. "You must be new indeed. The biotech biz is pretty incestuous, and yet I've never heard of you."

Cole grabbed the outstretched hand. Over the buzz of conversations, Alex swore she heard bones crunching.

"Well, Phil, you know how time flies when you're doing work you love. Having a great boss like Miss Kendall here makes me feel like I've only been on board a few days."

It was a bad time to try out the champagne. Alex sputtered, warm champagne bubbles scoring her throat and nose. Swallowing against the burn, she said, "I don't want to monopolize your time, Phillip. I'm sure you're just as eager to make contacts tonight as I am." She extended her hand in parting.

"Good meeting you too, Phil. Don't let us hold you up." Cole's "friendly" slap on the back knocked Phil a full step forward.

"Yeah, right." Shaking his Scotch-soaked cuff, Phillip backed away. "See you around the playground, Alex." He turned and walked away, his steps a lot less jaunty than when he'd approached.

Her gaze followed Philip across the room to the nearest bar. Being at close quarters with the man who'd very likely threatened her life was more unnerving than she'd anticipated.

Relieved to have a reprieve, she turned back to Cole. "Thank you. Even if we weren't competing for the same contract, he's a creep with a capital *C.*"

"You okay?" Like the question, his expression registered concern.

Feeling badly about having been so rude to him earlier, she lifted her gaze to his face. Damn, was it really necessary that he be quite so handsome? "I am now."

"That's good, real good."

He reached out a hand to her shoulder, his long fingers curling gently about the bone. It was very nearly the same spot Phillip had gone for, only Cole's touch brought a sense of familiarity and the dangerous temptation to give in, lean closer and accept the comfort he offered.

Feeling shaky, she stepped away. "I'd better go do my thing. It looks like the American ambassador has just been freed up, and I want to make sure I can count on his support."

Cole nodded, his gaze unnervingly locked on hers, the eye contact flooding her with five-year-old feelings that had no place in the present. "Don't worry about anything. I've got your back, okay."

"Okay." She turned to go, took a stumbling step forward, and then stopped to look back at him over her shoulder. Throat thick, she couldn't resist. "Just so you know…for the record, I'm really glad you're here tonight."

The warmth pooling in his eyes could have melted a glacier, only Alex had never felt less frozen in all her life. "For the record, so am I, Lex. So am I."

HE'D CALLED her Lex.

That had been his first mistake. His second had been to linger on the sofa in their suite's living room once they got back to the hotel. Instead, he should have excused himself and gone to bed. Except that a bodyguard couldn't retire and leave his principal still up and about. Seated on the cushion beside him, Alex was obviously too wired for sleep.

She shifted to face him. The jubilant smile she'd apparently been working at holding back broke over her face. "Three guesses who scored an 8:00 a.m. breakfast meeting with the Prime Minister at his private residence tomorrow morning?"

He'd seen her talking to the PM not long after the run-in with Collins. Cole couldn't be happier for her or prouder. "That's great. Congratulations." He reached out to give her a high five.

She turned to him, palm-up, and their hands met in a soft slap, her much smaller hand still the perfect mate to his. Taking it back, she admitted, "Now that the adrenaline rush is over, what I mostly am is hungry."

Their U.S. Embassy hosts had set out quite a spread. Early in the evening he'd seen her fill a plate from one of the buffet tables but, come to think of it, he'd never actually seen the food make it into her mouth.

"You didn't get anything to eat?" Neither had he, but that was beside the point.

She pulled out the pearl-studded hair clasp and combed her hand through her pale hair, the same phantom fingers he still sometimes felt raking down his back in dreams. "I had butterflies in my stomach the whole time. Scratch the butterflies, it felt more like bats. Wanna bet room service has signed off for the night?"

Given that it was after ten, and Belmopan more or less rolled up the sidewalks by eight-thirty, Cole conceded it was a pretty good call. "The lobby bar is open until eleven. We can grab something there." Meeting her questioning look, he admitted, "Yes, I checked the hours earlier. You know me. It's all about the logistics."

She was already slipping her shoes back on. "In that case, let's do it. Now that I'm officially off duty until tomorrow morning, I want a real drink, too, a stiff one, with ice—lots of ice."

A stiff one—God, if she only knew. He cast a self-conscious glance down to the front of his pants. Fortunately his tuxedo jacket was long enough to partially cover what he was sure must be a full-fledged woody.

With her loose hair waving around her shoulders and that adorably silly grin on her face, she looked so much like the Alex of five years ago he almost did a double take.

So she hadn't forgotten how to smile after all.

She reached for him, her slender hand wrapping around his wrist and tugging him toward the door. There was no way she could have begun to budge him, but she didn't have to. He was more than willing to follow her anywhere—New York, Belize, the jaws of Hell. So long as she looked up at him with those laughing honey-brown eyes and that sexy carefree smile, he didn't care where they went or when or if they came back.

With her hand cuffing him, for the time being he gave himself up to the insanity. "Okay, okay, I'm sold. I'm *there.* Just promise me this time you won't eat the worm."

7

DIMLY LIT and nearly deserted, the lobby lounge turned out to be the perfect chill spot. Votive candles lined the bar. The staff still on duty consisted of a bartender and a DJ spinning Punta Rock covers. A young couple, clearly locals, burned up the dance floor, their dirty dancing settling into a butt-to-groin grind that had Alex reaching for her chilled bottle of water and avoiding Cole's gaze.

"Honeymooners," the bartender intoned, shooting a wink. He cleared away their plates and set down their second round of drinks—rum punch for her, punch and soda for him.

Alex dared a glance at her "drinking buddy." Seated on the stool beside her, Cole batted the votive candle between his hands hockey-puck fashion across the varnished bar top. His first drink was still more than half full, the melting ice turning the deep berry red to pale pink.

Alex had never known him to be so fidgety—or so quiet. Since they'd come downstairs a half hour before, his responses so far were "yes," "no," and "sure, that sounds good to me."

He was probably just tired and hot, she told herself. Even though she was more lightly dressed, the lined linen clung to her damp skin, the backs of her bare legs sticking to the vinyl bar seat. Being buttoned into a tuxedo in tropical temperatures must be way more miserable. At her urging, he'd left his tuxedo jacket upstairs in the room. His loosened bow tie hung at half mast, the starched fabric drooping in the heat, and his shirtsleeves were rolled up beyond his elbows. His forearms rested on the edge of the bar, corded with muscle and dusted with dark hair. A stain of perspiration spread between his shoulder blades, causing the shirt to cling to his broad back. Sitting so close she could…dear God, she could smell him. And he smelled really good, mouthwatering good, a sensuously musky mix of shower gel and aftershave, and yes, just the right amount of sweat.

Throat dry, she uncapped her water bottle and took another long drink. "You broke our rule."

"What rule is that?" He gave the votive a rest and looked over at her.

"You know, the really important one about not bringing up the past."

His expression was a question mark. "I committed this alleged rule breakage recently?"

"That comment about me eating the tequila worm, it really…it really took me back."

Shit, why had she gone and admitted that? Talk about wearing her heart on her sleeve. She reached for her drink, a fruity concoction of the local coconut rum with *volcano* in the name and apparently truth serum as its principal ingredient.

The night she and Cole had first met in Denver, her friends had talked her into doing tequila shots. It was supposed to have been just the one round to ring in the Big 3-0, a benchmark birthday. After the second round, and with two beers under her belt already, the bar had begun to seesaw. With Jaime and Brenda egging her on, eating the worm from the bottom of the bottle suddenly seemed like a really good idea—going home with the hunky cowboy singer with the ice-blue eyes and hot body an even better one. She'd ended the evening by getting sick all over Cole's bathroom, but not before they'd had some really amazing sex.

"I'm sorry," he said, looking almost as though he meant it. "It wasn't deliberate. Whenever tequila comes up, so to speak, I can't help thinking of you." Breaking into a broad grin, he tossed back his head and laughed.

Alex couldn't help it. She laughed with him. "Too bad you opted for spook. I think you might have missed your calling as a stand-up comic."

As though she'd doused him with the rest of the water in her bottle, he suddenly sobered. "I've missed out on a lot of things." He pivoted in his seat toward her.

And just like that the mood shifted—and the heat spiked. Out on the dance floor, the music segued to a slow song, the couple's movements winding down with it. Perspiration glistened on their scantily clad bodies. The young woman's slender brown arms twined about her new husband's neck, her breasts brushing the dark skin showing through his half-open shirt, her swaying hips anchored to his gyrating pelvis by his spread hands. Alex swallowed hard. Once she and Cole had moved together like that. The song had been Dan Hill's "Sometimes When We Touch," the bar had been the one in snowy Denver, not steamy Belize, and though Hill's lyrics might come off as cornball to some, it all had been perfect, absolutely perfect.

Cheeks on fire, Alex swung back around to Cole. His gaze raked over her face, settling on her mouth. The starkness in those blue depths had her gasping. Her chest felt tight, her breasts unbearably heavy. Because of her almost backless dress, she hadn't been able to wear so much as a strapless bra. She'd settled for the cover-ups called "petals," but the fragile floral discs were no match for her hardening nipples.

She wet her dry lips, wishing she'd asked for more ice in her drink. "It's late. I really should—"

He cut her off with a shake of his head. "Take a walk with me."

"It's late," she repeated. Moisture that had nothing to do with the heat pooled between her thighs. In contrast, the inside of her mouth felt as dry as the desert.

Pulling out his money clip, he tossed notes on the bar. "Take a walk with me anyway." He got up from the stool and held out his hand.

Alex hesitated and then slid her hand into his. The sliding glass doors leading out to the patio had been left open. They walked through. Floodlights illuminated the cabana bar and pool. Flowering plants in decorative clay pots sat at intervals along the periphery. Hibiscus, iris, lobster claw and red ginger released their ripe fragrances into the syrupy air. In the distance, palm fronds swayed below a star-studded canopy untouched by ambient light.

Cole slid his arm around Alex's waist. She knew she should move away and yet she didn't want to. He maneuvered them out of eyeshot of the glass doors and turned her to face him. His glancing touch on her bare arms raised gooseflesh; his eyes on her mouth had her forgetting to breathe.

"You're so beautiful." He leaned into her, close enough that she could smell the fruity punch on his breath. "Would you believe that after all these years, I still remember how amazing you taste?" His voice was a warm whisper in her ear; his eyes blue firelight, his moist mouth a hairsbreadth away. "What about you, Lex? Do you still remember how good we were together?"

Five years of longing welled up inside her. Her eyes misted, her mouth trembled. She nodded. "Of course, I remember." How could she not?

He reached out, framing her face between his big gentle hands. "What would you say if I told you I still have feelings for you? What would you say if I told you a day hasn't gone by since I last saw you that I haven't thought of you and wondered if you were happy? Where you were?"

Feeling as though the thick air were bearing down on her, Alex bit her lip. "I'd say you were five years too late."

"Look at me." He slid his knuckles beneath her chin and brought her face close to his. "You're not the only one who's changed. I'm not the same single-minded man who left you at the airport five years ago. I'm not that guy anymore, Lex."

She blinked away tears. "How can I trust that? How can I trust you?"

"Maybe you should start by trusting yourself."

In a heartbeat, the past five years fell away, leaving nothing but this moment, this man and the aching need to be with him. Alex tipped her face the final few inches up to his. Her hand found the back of his neck. Even in high heels, she had to rise up on her toes to meet him. Their mouths met, melded. Like their hands, their lips were still the perfect match.

He brushed his mouth over her closed one, his one hand sliding up the sensitized flesh of her throat to cradle her cheek. "Alex." He teased his tongue along the seam of her still-closed lips, and she parted for him like a flower.

After five years of unquenched thirst she drank him in. The kiss turned hungry, demanding. She lifted her other arm from her side and anchored it to the shelf of one broad shoulder, sinking her nails into the cloth of his sweat-damp shirt. She'd forgotten how lean he was, how steely hard.

She pulled away and lowered her head to lay a trail of lapping, nipping kisses alongside his neck. His skin was salt-flavored, damp and utterly delicious, the corded muscles of his throat working against her mouth. Memories flooded her, drenching her body in desire. Remembering, she slid one hand from his shoulder to his chest, smoothing the sculpted planes of his pectorals with her palm, her thumb playing with his nipple through the cotton. He'd always been sensitive there.

He jerked back hard and speared a hand through the fall of her hair, his fingers tunneling through the loose waves, the tips scraping against her scalp. "Lex."

With his other hand he cupped her breast, thumb flicking the tip. Wetness splashed the space between her thighs, setting the tender skin to throbbing. Like the young woman on the dance floor inside, she ground against him, craving connection with his hardness, his heat. Still kissing her, he backed them up, farther away from the door. Her butt bumped up against one of the wrought-iron patio tables. Braced against the edge, she dragged his hand downward.

"Cole." She was close to coming, so very close.

He slid his hand beneath her dress, the heat of his palm branding the inside of her thigh. He edged upward, fingertips brushing the edge of her panties. He stopped and looked up at her, his eyes silently questioning. She answered with a moan and covered her hand over his, pressing him closer. He moved the strip of lace aside and found her with his fingers. Sticky heat blanketed her thighs, his hand working against her the closest she'd come to heaven in five years. She felt her muscles contract against his fingers. The scent of her arousal rose up between them, her musk mingling with the dizzying fragrance of flowers. And suddenly she was drowning, going under, her breath and her sanity slipping beneath the heat and the madness.

She came, exploded. The contractions struck hard and deep, deeper than she'd ever known or imagined. At the last, she cried out, the music from inside the bar drowning her release.

He pulled her dress down and rested his damp forehead against hers. "Come to bed with me, Lex. If nothing else, I'll be happy just to hold you."

From within, the house lights came on, the sudden neon brightness striking through the glass. Cole whirled to the door, blocking her with his body, though it turned out there was no one there to see.

Alex slid off the table to stand on wobbly legs, her fogged brain suddenly registering what she'd done.

Cursing beneath his breath, Cole swung around to face her. "Come to bed with me. I promise you won't be sorry. I promise it will be like it was five years ago only better. I promise tonight won't be the end. There doesn't have to be an end, not this time."

He reached to take her in his arms, but she warded him off with a hand to his chest. Tears welled in her eyes. She shook her head, sending one fat droplet flying. "I've learned the hard way your promises don't amount to much."

Way to go, Romeo.

Cole stepped inside the suite's living room a few minutes later. Stagnant air hit him in the face. He'd meant to stop by the front desk and tell the clerk about the air conditioner, but in the throes of all the drama he'd forgotten. He slammed his keys atop the TV console and crossed the room. Hot, sweaty and with a turbo-charged erection weighing between his legs, he felt like shit. The short, silent walk from the lounge through the lobby had felt like a funeral procession. Once inside the elevator, Alex had fumbled for her key and refused to look his way. Of course, he hadn't let that stop him.

"Talk to me, Alex."

Her head had shot up, the hurt look in her eyes slashing at his heart like a razor. "If I go to bed with you now, it would be five years ago all over again, and frankly I'm not up for that."

He dragged a hand through his damp hair. "According to my memory, five years ago was pretty damned amazing."

"Not at the end, it wasn't." Back to the elevator wall, she frowned over at him, the effect slightly ruined by her kiss-swollen lips. "I gave you my whole heart, and you broke it. I deserved better. How can I ever trust you again? How can you even ask me to?"

Guilt rushed him and tenderness, too. He stepped closer. "Your heart's not broken, baby. It's wounded, and even the worst wounds heal with time. Let me make it up to you. C'mon, Lex, what do you have to lose?"

"Other than my future, you mean? Not a thing."

Cole froze. He let his hands drop to his sides. By "future," she meant marriage to Traxton, of course. "You're right, you do deserve better than me, a lot better. You're smart, talented and drop-dead gorgeous. The whole corporate-mogul thing notwithstanding, I'm just not sold on Traxton as the better alternative."

She bristled. "You don't know him like I do. Randall is considerate and caring and he wants a family."

He grabbed her by the shoulders. He didn't shake her, but he wanted to. "But does he turn you on? Do you get wet thinking about him?" Jesus, where had that come from?

The elevator doors opened. She jerked away as though he'd burned her. "Being happy with someone involves a lot more than just sex, Cole."

She stepped off and stalked down the hallway to their suite. Still her bodyguard, he had no real choice but to follow her, reaching the door in time to have it thrown closed in his face.

Crossing the carpet, he started stripping off his shirt, definitely on the ripe side and ready for the cleaner's. He briefly considered going back downstairs and getting shit-faced. But asleep or not, safe or not, nice to him or not, Alex Kendall was still his responsibility, his job, his mission. Duty aside, going on a binge held zero appeal. Maybe it was because he was getting older, but slamming down large quantities of alcohol only seemed to make a bad situation worse.

He eyed the connecting door, the flimsy-looking deadbolt chain on his side hanging at half mast. He wondered if she'd slid the chain across on her side. He couldn't blame her if she had. What he'd pulled downstairs was the equivalent of taking a wrecking ball to her newly built, bright shiny life. By the looks of it, she had a good thing going with Traxton. Who was he to tell her to throw that away for…*what?* The week after next he'd be in Mogadishu. Assuming he got back alive, who was to say where he'd be the next month or the month after that?

He might still lead a nomad's life, but he liked to think he'd changed from five years ago, grown at least, mellowed certainly. For sure he wasn't the same hotheaded idiot who'd let self-pity and a kid's taunts lead him stupidly astray. God knew he was as stubborn as ever and, yes, still ambitious. He fully intended to steer Guidepost to the next level, but being recognized as a security guru among America's corporate elite no longer felt like enough. He couldn't go on living for work. He wanted, needed, to carve out something for himself, and that elusive "something" centered on having a special lady to love and plan a future with. It centered on Alex. The episode by the pool had raised his hopes that he had a shot at getting her back. This was Alex, after all. She couldn't be happy with Traxton and still do…*that* with Cole.

Alex was the hands-down best thing that had ever happened to him, but five years ago he'd blown it. For whatever reason—God, Fate, or pure luck—he'd been given a second chance with her in the form of four steamy days and tropical nights.

Feeling more optimistic, he headed into the bathroom. Still tense and turned on from the episode downstairs, he really needed a shower before bed. His earlier one had been lightning quick and disappointingly tepid. He crossed his fingers that this time the pipes would cooperate and serve it up icy cold.

Denver 2003

COLE'S GAZE homed in on the beautiful blond birthday girl nursing her second tequila shot and pretending to talk to her friends. Her mouth might be moving a mile a minute, but he didn't miss how her eyes never left his face. And suddenly Cole knew that this was one of those times in life when you just had to go for it. He gave up his guitar to a startled Special Agent McKenzie, his second string, and strode down the stage steps.

Reaching her table yet again, he bent to her ear. "Dance with me." He held out his hand.

Alex shot frantic looks between her two girlfriends, but they'd had way more to drink than she had and were already on his side.

The redhead nudged Alex out of her seat. "Go for it, girl-friend. It's your frickin' thirtieth birthday."

"Yeah, Lexie," the brunette chimed in. "It's vacation. Have some fun."

"Okay, okay, I will." She pushed back from the table. "I'd love to dance, thank you." Lifting shy eyes to his face, she took his hand and stood.

Feeling as though he'd just conquered earth, Cole threaded his fingers through her slender ones and led her out onto the floor. Minus the stupid disco globe twirling above them, his arms closing around her was the most perfect moment of his life, her head tucked against his chest the closest he'd ever felt to coming home.

"Happy birthday, beautiful," he whispered into her ear, and he sensed he wasn't only meant to celebrate this birthday with her but all the rest, too.

8

THE SENSE of being watched drew Cole out of the memory-dream of Alex, who else? He came awake to a King Kong-size hard-on and the equivalent of an ice-cream headache in his balls.

Adrenaline kicking in, he jolted upright and reached into the night-table drawer for his pistol. Backlit by the ceiling light in her room, Alex stepped inside his room. Her pale hair hung in loose waves around her shoulders and an oversized T-shirt barely covered her butt.

"What the fuck…"

"I knocked but I guess you didn't hear me."

He slid the pistol back in the drawer and slammed it. "Jesus, don't you know better than to sneak up on a sniper when he's sleeping? I could have shot you. You could be dead right now."

She bit her bottom lip. He couldn't say why, but he'd always found the mannerism incredibly erotic. "I didn't think about that. I thought you were still up. I thought I heard you calling my name and…" Her voice trailed off, which was just as well.

He scraped a hand through his hair, absorbing the shock. He'd called out her name in his sleep—talk about humiliating. "Well, you heard wrong."

"I guess so. I'm sorry I disturbed you." Backing up to the door, she gave the tail of the T-shirt a futile tug. "I'll let you get back to sleep."

Get back to sleep, right! The chance of that happening anytime soon was on par with snowballs surviving hell and pigs taking up flying. "Now that we're here and both awake, you might as well tell me what's up."

Nice choice of words, Whittaker—not. He was up, that's what, and if not for the blanket bunched around his waist, that embarrassing fact would be all too evident.

She drew in a visibly deep breath and slowly walked toward the bed. Heart pounding, Cole watched her. With each successive step she took toward him, he forgot to think, forgot to breathe, forgot to do anything beyond focus on Alex approaching.

She stopped short of bumping up against the side of the mattress. "I've been thinking about what happened earlier… you know…by the, uh…pool."

As if he could forget. As if he needed her to point out co-ordinates on a map as a reminder.

She chewed her bottom lip so hard it couldn't help but hurt. "Being here with you like this makes me realize I've never really gotten over you."

His heart soared. He turned to her, arms lifting. "Baby, I—"

Her head shake silenced him. "Please, Cole, let me finish." She sat on the side of his bed without waiting to be asked. "After we came back upstairs and I got to my room and cooled off, it hit me. Before the anger and hurt can go away, I really need to get you out of my system."

His heart dropped a notch. Watching her face closely for cues, he said, "Define getting me out of your system."

She brightened as though a light bulb had gone on inside her. "You and me, one blow-out sexual binge from now until we land back in New York on Friday. But once we land, it's over. We walk away and go our separate ways, no strings and no promises, which means there can't be any regrets or hard feelings, either. Think you can handle that?"

If the devil had set out to trap him into selling his soul, ol' Lucifer couldn't have come up with a better bargain. He shrugged, though his chest suddenly felt as tight as his drawn-up balls. "I'm a guy, remember? Sex without strings is practically programmed into my DNA."

She rolled her eyes. "I figured as much."

In the short term, the one downside to their arrangement was he only had a single "emergency" condom with him. Then again, maybe she was on the pill. He considered asking about her birth control status, then decided against it. They hadn't seen each other for five years, and she had every right to expect him to use a condom. Beyond that, he didn't want to make her any more uncomfortable than she already was. Now that her bold speech was over, he could sense the tension coming off her in waves.

He lifted the covers to let her in. "Come here, you."

She looked down and her mouth fell open. "I guess I forgot…" Her voice broke off. Too late he remembered pulling off his boxers before climbing into bed. He followed her wide-eyed gaze to the nearly nine inches of him standing at full attention. He was rock-hard and throbbing, almost painfully erect. Beyond taking care of business earlier in the shower, he hadn't given much thought to a sexual outlet, a flesh-and-blood lover, in some time. He dragged in a mouthful of muggy air and willed his hyper-charged body to dial it down. He'd fantasized about this reunion for five years, and now that the moment was here, he meant for it to last longer than five minutes—a lot longer.

She slipped into bed beside him. He wrapped his arm around her, and she settled in with a sigh. He was amazed that after five years it could feel so natural to hold her, so com-

pletely comfortable and, yes, right. He remembered everything about her from before, every lush curve and alluring
angle and shadowed hollow. He remembered the soft sounds
she made when she was building toward climax and the deep,
throaty cries she let out once she made it there. He remembered how she loved it when he traced the curve of her spine
with his fingers and then turned her on her front and pressed
open-mouth kisses to the cheeks of her tight, white ass. He
remembered every searching glance and satisfied sound and
sexy endearment—and he couldn't wait to experience them
all firsthand again.

He eased her onto her back. Lying beside her, he braced
his weight on one elbow and smoothed his other hand over
her breasts.

He found her nipple through the cotton cloth of her T-shirt,
and she shivered. "I might need some time to, you know, get
used to you again."

He stilled his hand. "Hey, it's me, remember? I'm not
going to do anything you don't want."

She smiled up at him, the lost look on her face catching
at his heart. "How could you when there's nothing I don't
want us to do."

Nothing left…a lot. He could kick himself for not stocking
up on condoms.

As if reading his mind, she said, "I, uh…have a confession
to make. I brought condoms with me. It's not what you're
thinking. I went off the pill last month, and so I bought this
box just to keep…on hand. It's never even been opened…I
tossed it in my toiletry bag and—"

Feeling as though Christmas had come early, he laid a
finger across her lips. "You don't have to explain yourself to
me. I'm just glad I get to love you as many times as we want."

She smiled up at him and he got a glimpse of the old Alex in her impish grin and mischievous eyes. "In that case, you'd better get busy."

Cole got busy.

He lifted her arms over her head and pulled the T-shirt off. There was no need to relearn the terrain. It was basically the same body, the same Alex he'd made love to five years ago— and a hundred thousand times since in his mind. Milky skin stretched over long, delicate bones. Small, perfectly proportioned breasts, slightly fuller than before but still crowned with pale-pink areolas and luscious long nipples. The well of her flat stomach was still the perfect fit for his palm. Sliding his hand downward, he traced the lacy top of her panties, a prelude to taking them off. She lifted her hips for him and he slid them down her long legs and then off.

"Alex."

He eased her thighs apart and stared down at her, a mouth-watering sight. He hadn't exaggerated earlier when he'd said he still remembered the taste of her. What he hadn't said was he remembered her scent too, a cross between freshly mowed grass and that first summertime salty breath of the sea. And she was still the same pretty pink, the outer lips dusky, the inner ones a rich raspberry, all of her delicious. He'd never stopped loving her, and though he'd tried telling himself he must have idealized her in ways large and small, that she couldn't possibly be as amazing as he remembered, being with her again disproved both arguments.

Kneeling, he sat back on his heels to look at her, just look at her. "Alex, you're beautiful. You really are."

She smiled up at him. "So are you."

And he was, more beautiful than she'd remembered, which was saying a lot. She reached up and ran her palm over his chest, the sculpted planes dusted with dark hair and rippling with muscle. Lifting her head, she drew the disk of one flat brownish-pink nipple into her mouth.

Cole groaned. He sucked in his breath. "Easy, baby. Right now this is all about you."

He left her and slid downward. His hands, warm, strong, and knowing, found the inside of her thighs, pulling them apart. "I can't wait to taste you." Far from waiting, he lowered his head, his big, gentle hands pulling her nether lips apart. Lapping at her labia, he stopped to look up at her. "I've always loved the way you taste." His breath was a jet of steam striking the damp inside of her thighs. "For years I used to wake up with a hard-on from dreaming about going down on you."

He touched his tongue to her clit, and she fisted her hands in the sheet. She speared her fingers through his hair and held him there for one sinfully long moment.

"I know. I feel the same way about you. Only, Cole, please, as amazing as this feels, I don't want to wait any longer."

Cole didn't need to be asked a second time. He reached across her to the drawer and brought out his toiletry bag and, she guessed, the condom. The foil packet glinted in the low light. He tried tearing it open, first with his fingers, and then his teeth. It finally tore free, the prophylactic zinging across the bed like a missile.

In the dim light, she thought she saw his ears go red. "Sorry, that was clumsy of me."

"No, that was real life." She pushed up on her elbows and retrieved it. "Here, let me."

Rolling on the condom was more about touching him than anything else. Long, thick and perfectly formed, he was beautiful here, too, and his musky scent brought back all kinds of memories, only good ones. Her mouth watered, her sex pulsed. She dipped her head to draw him into her mouth but his hands were on her shoulders, easing her back onto the pillows.

She opened her legs, inviting him inside, secretly wishing he would want to stay with her like this for more than a meager four days. He entered her in one sweepingly beautiful thrust that stole her breath and had her anchoring her knees to his lean hips. She'd forgotten how amazing it was having him inside her. She hadn't felt so full, so complete, in five years. He started to move, striking deeply within. The sensation was almost too much, too good to last for long. She was going to come, not only hard but quickly, far too soon.

Cole pulled out of her, teasing her clit with his head. Reaching down, he followed with his finger. "Let it go, Alex. Let yourself go and just fall. I promise this time I'll be there to catch you."

He stroked into her again, and Alex came apart, shattered into a million little pieces, each shard radiating an incredible thrumming heat that began in her core and traveled to the nerve endings of her fingertips and toes. When she came to, he still filled her, her body and yes, her heart. But leaps of faith went two ways. Looking up into Cole's taut face, she reached down between them and palmed his balls.

He started moving again, so hard and fast that if she hadn't been drenched it would have hurt her. It didn't hurt though, and even if it had she wouldn't have stopped him. She dug her nails into the taut muscles of his backside as he poured into her, drinking in each delicious shudder, wishing for once he would let go all the way, throw back his head and scream.

He buried his head in the curve of her neck and shuddered while she held onto him with both arms.

I'm happy, she thought, and squeezed her eyes closed to

block out anything but the bliss. *I'm happy like I never thought to be happy again. I'm happy, honest-to-God happy. It's been so long I'd almost forgotten what it feels like to be happy, to just let go.*

And she was happy, for the moment at least. Too bad there was no way the moment could last.

3:15 a.m.

"IT'S NOT FAIR, you know."

Cole cracked open an eye to find Alex wide awake and watching him. "What's not fair, baby?"

Resting her weight on one elbow, Alex lay on her side, her hair tickling his chest. She used one of her long, elegant fingers to trace the contours of his face. "How beautiful you are. You're even handsomer than you were five years ago. I like you with the gray."

Though he'd been sound asleep, dead to the world, he couldn't help but chuckle. "Good thing you told me. I was just about to break out the Grecian Formula."

His smart-ass comment had her smiling, something he hoped to see a whole lot more of over the next few days. Sliding a hand between them, she lightly scratched the underside of his shaft with her fingernail. "You were always so quiet when you came. You still are. You hardly make a sound."

Cole leaned over and kissed the tip of her nose. "Old habits die hard."

How could he tell her that even in the midst of a life-or-death mission, men were still men? They still thought about sex, if not exactly all the time, then at least a hell of a lot. When taking care of bodily needs in close quarters, you learned to do so quickly, efficiently and above all silently.

He covered her hand with his and pressed against her palm. "Just because I don't shout out to the rooftop doesn't mean you aren't making me crazy. The way you touch me, it blows my mind. And it hasn't changed. I thought it would have, but it hasn't. If anything it's even better than I remember." Lifting his head, he glanced down at their joined hands, her slender fingers furling about his penis, already hard again. "Right now what you're doing, touching me like that, it's *killing* me."

Alex cut him a wicked look. "Look on the bright side. At least you'll die smiling."

He flopped back onto the pillows with a groan. "I'll die rock-hard."

She let go and slid down the length of him. "I won't torture you that badly."

He sucked in a breath as her thumb found the slit at the head of his cock, sliding back and forth in the stickiness.

"Let me take you some place, okay?" She brushed her mouth over his.

Against her open lips, he whispered, "I'll let you take me anywhere you want. I'll *do* anything you want."

She lifted a light-brown brow. "Anything?"

He didn't hesitate. If she wanted him as her personal sex slave, he was more than happy to sign up. "Anything, you name it."

"In that case, roll over on your stomach."

As kink went, a back rub was pretty vanilla, but he was more than willing to go along with whatever she had planned. She used to bring her scented massage oils with her when she'd visited him in Denver. She'd been into aromatherapy in a big way back then. As for him, he'd been into her. He'd let her rub any number of floral fragrances into him, from lavender to jasmine to, well…after a while, it all smelled the same. So long as her hands were doing the massaging, he hadn't cared if he did smell like a pansy.

Those same slender, capable hands now slid lower, kneading his buttocks, the backs of his thighs. She slid clever fingers between his cheeks, tracing the sensitive juncture, toying with the ring of puckered flesh.

Cole's head shot up from the pillow. He didn't remember her doing that before.

He looked back at her over one shoulder. "What the hell?"

She smiled at him. "You like that, don't you?"

He probably shouldn't, but the truth was he did—a lot. "You're getting me excited all over again."

His cock was board-stiff against the mattress, but then his body had always been an open book to her, his thoughts, too. Right now the movie reel he was rolling out in his mind's eye was definitely triple-X, complete with Surround Sound and hi-def.

"Good."

The pinch of teeth sinking into his ass took him by surprise. "Holy—!" He twisted his head to look back at her.

"Too much? Sorry." She smiled, not looking sorry at all.

He felt the brush of long silky hair on his back and then the wet tickle of her tongue sliding upwards along his lower spine. He didn't remember her being this bold, but he was more than ready to embrace this aspect of the new her. Still playing with his ass, she slid her tongue from just above his coccyx to midway up his spine, a slow, seductive glide. He looked down and saw a bead of come soak into the bottom sheet, another first for him—so much for his prized self-control.

He rolled onto his back. Reaching up, he anchored his hands to her hips and pulled her down on top of him. "I'm sorry, baby. I can't take any more—and I can't wait."

"Too bad because you're going to have to. Lie back."

She slammed slender hands against his chest and shoved him back into the mattress. He could have resisted easily, but he found himself loving this new, edgy side to her. The role-playing, coupled with the soft touch and tight body he knew so well, made for one sexy combination.

"Put your hands over your head." The husky command could have come from a professional dominatrix. "Good." Her hold slipped away. "Keep them there. I'll be right back."

She left the bed for a fraction of a minute, just long enough for him to wonder what she was up to. Watching her walk toward him, her lithe body backlit by the bathroom light and her slim sexy hips swaying, he was aware that his pulse had quickened and so had his breathing. As for his cock, it stuck up from his groin like an arrow pointed due north.

The mattress dipped slightly as she joined him once more. "Miss me?" The question came out as a husky purr.

She secured him not with silk scarves or Velcro wrist cuffs but with a practical item at hand, the belt of the complimentary guest bathrobe. She used the terry-cloth tie to bind his wrists to the rusting metal posts. They'd probably both need tetanus shots once they were back in the States, but for now any risk seemed totally worth it.

She didn't need makeshift manacles to overcome his self-control. One long, lingering look from her brown eyes was all it took to melt him.

She settled back on her heels and stared down at him. Her breasts, fuller than five years ago, dangled in his face, the taut nipples bare inches from his mouth. Mouth watering, he brought his head up from the pillow but at the last minute she pulled back with a shake of her head.

"I've never seen you helpless before. I think I could learn to like you this way."

He was so hard, so full that he bit the inside of his cheek to keep from succumbing and simply letting go. "Just remember, Lex, paybacks are hell."

A wicked smile brought up the corners of her beautiful, kissable mouth. "You can tie me up later if you want…if you have anything left, that is." Holding his gaze, she arched her back and circled her nipples with the pads of her thumbs.

Another bead of come slid down the side of him. He sank his teeth into his bottom lip and willed himself to stay focused, to stay strong.

"Oh, I'll have plenty left, don't you worry." How he hoped that would be the case. He was so turned on, he felt like a bomb about to detonate. "For right now, though, straddle my face."

Her caressing hands stalled in mid-stroke. Raised brows greeted that suggestion. "You don't mind my, uh…using you like that?"

Mind! Was she kidding? The thought of serving as her private sex slave was the king of turn-ons.

He shook his head. "My mouth is watering just thinking how good you're going to taste."

She swung one beautiful long leg over him and shimmied up his torso, planted a knee outside either of his shoulders, and settled herself over him, but not before he caught her wince. He had very broad shoulders and she had very slender hips. The position spread her thighs as far apart as they could go. Pulled like a wishbone, she was completely open to him, the petals of her vagina glistening in the semi-darkness, the triangle of coarse curls above likewise drenched with dew.

Musk filled his senses. He shifted his shoulders, locking her in place. She bit her bottom lip but didn't budge. "I've waited five years for this." Lifting his head, he breathed deeply and buried himself in her heat.

Whatever discomfort she'd felt before seemed to melt away the moment he opened his mouth to take her. "Oh, Cole." She rolled her hips, bringing velvet slick folds flush with his mouth.

The first sweep of his tongue had her grabbing the bedposts and grinding against him. She tasted even better than she had earlier, earthy and just a little bit ripe.

With the tip of his tongue he circled the kernel of her clitoris, circled and then retreated, again and again until her hips moved in rhythm with his stroking, her whimpering confirming that bound or not he was back in command.

"Oh, Cole, oh…Cole!" Tossing back her head, she slammed against him, driving the bed into the wall.

Rich cream spurted into his mouth. Tender flesh trembled against lips and tongue. Taut as guitar strings, the muscles of her inner thighs shuddered against his shoulders. He felt a tickling sensation around his ribs and realized sweat—his, hers, theirs—must be trickling down his sides.

Above him, Alex gasped, "Cole, please… Please…stop. I really need you to…stop—now!"

He didn't answer, not with words. Instead he kept tonguing her, stroke after stroke, determined to splinter her self-control, pull her apart. No matter how much she begged him, he refused to relent, not until she came a second time.

Whether they had four days together or forty years, he meant to make memories with her that would last a lifetime.

4:00 a.m.

AFTERWARD someone had to break the tension piling up between them. Alex figured it might as well be her, but Cole beat her to the punch. "I don't remember us doing *that* five years ago. I wouldn't have thought we could top the good ol' days, but I was wrong."

So, he'd liked it. That was...interesting. Better than interesting, it was good. But then maybe he'd just liked doing it in general versus doing it with her specifically. That prospect had her feeling far less happy.

As a writer, make that *former* writer, she had a pretty rich interior world. From time to time she'd fantasized some light S&M scenarios. And yet she'd never come close to doing... *that* with any lover before, certainly not with Randall. Her fiancé was controlling enough in daily life without contriving special scenarios. He was too much of a control freak to consider letting someone else be in charge even if that someone else was a lover he meant to marry.

She must not be as sophisticated as she liked to think, because even though she and Cole had no future beyond the next four, now three, days, she wanted to believe what they shared was unique, maybe even once-in-a-lifetime. But then, where Cole was concerned she'd always been a fool, a fool for love.

"You never married?" Not trusting herself to look at him, she lifted her eyes to the ceiling and held them there.

"Nope."

One loaded question from her had brought them down to single-word, single-syllable answers. Great.

Focusing on the cracked plaster, she asked, "Do you, uh... have you... Do you have a lot of girlfriends?" In one short stammering sentence she'd shot backward in time from junior prom to, roughly speaking, eighth grade.

In the semi-darkness, she heard him draw a deep breath. "Not a lot."

"Not a lot" wasn't the same thing as "a few," or better yet, "none," but she supposed it was the best she could hope for. Cole was a former FBI agent, after all. He may have left the Agency, but he was still in a similar line of work. As the CEO of a global security firm, action-adventure was practically his middle name. Like James Bond, he probably had women scattered like seed crop all around the country— make that, globe.

And then he startled her by asking, "What about you… other than Traxton, I mean?"

The latter part of the question reminded her that if either of them was acting in the wrong, it was her. She turned her head to face him. "Not a lot? Why?"

"For one thing, you travel with a box of condoms, not that I'm knocking you for it. I'm all for being responsible."

The condoms, damn! She almost hadn't mentioned them, but that would have meant forgoing intercourse with Cole. Given how little time they had together, that would have been a shame.

"Like I told you, I bought that box after I went off the pill last month. I wanted to start getting my body regulated to…try and have a baby after the…wedding."

His expression shuttered and he went the equivalent of radio silent, not that she blamed him. Chatting up your future husband to your lover—talk about a libido buster.

Regretting having started down this path, she lifted her head from his pillow onto her own. "I have an early day tomorrow—make that today." She hesitated, wondering whether she should kiss him.

"We both have an early day." His gaze met hers in the semi-darkness. "I'm your bodyguard, remember? Where you go, I go."

"In that case, I guess we'd both better grab some sleep."

She turned onto her side, not really surprised to feel a trickle of wetness on her cheek. Cole's lips brushing over her shoulder seemed a bittersweet end to the evening. Paybacks were hell—only she hadn't expected to have to start anteing up until after they left Belize.

9

"I WAS IN the middle of the most amazing dream," Alex announced roughly five minutes after Cole reached across her and shut off the snooze button on the radio alarm.

It was after eight, decadently late by his usual standards and hers, too, or so he suspected. The Prime Minister's executive secretary had called at seven to express His Honor's regrets that he wouldn't be able to meet with Alex over breakfast after all. Alex hadn't liked the sound of that. Had Phillip somehow gotten to him or was it a simple scheduling conflict as the secretary insisted? Whichever, forcing the issue wasn't going to get her anywhere. She still had the presentation to the cabinet that afternoon. It was her best shot at recovering any lost ground.

Her ordinary response would be to lace up her running shoes and hit the road, logging in mile after sweaty mile until she exhausted herself. Instead, she'd snuggled up to Cole and slept for another whole hour.

"Oh, yeah?" He rolled onto his side and pulled her against him. "A sexy dream?"

"Uh-huh." She nuzzled his neck. "A *very* sexy dream."

He leaned over her. "Was I in it?"

She smiled, finding his fishing to be really endearing, totally cute. "You were definitely a...major player. Okay, you were the lead. You might say you have a lot to live up to."

Burying his grin in the curve of her neck, he slid his hand beneath the sheet and cupped her breast. "Hold that thought for another thirty minutes." He planted a smacker on her forehead and rolled out of bed.

She elbowed her way upright. "Hey, in case you missed the hint, that was a definite proposition."

"Hold that thought then, until I get back." He stood by the closed door pulling on a T-shirt over the jeans he'd yet to zipper. His hair was mussed and his left cheek wore a pillow crease. God, he was gorgeous. "I need to hook us up with a decent car and some AC. I'll pick up breakfast while I'm out. What would you like?"

She propped a second pillow behind her and lay back. "I'd rather have you for breakfast."

Had she really just said that? Whatever "it" was, Cole certainly brought it out in her. She'd never dream of saying something so brazen to Randall.

A pang of guilt hit her. Randall might not be Prince Charming, but he deserved better from her than being cheated on. She wasn't kidding herself. Whether she and Cole were star-crossed lovers or two people who'd gotten swept up in the nostalgia of a reunion fling, whatever they shared was for the present, specifically three days counting this one. Still, she couldn't see how she could go through with marrying Randall now. She hadn't been able to promise undying love before, but she had meant to give him her fidelity. Without even that, what foundation was there for a marriage?

Her darkening thoughts must have been mirrored on her

face. Cole shoved his wallet into the back pocket of his jeans and crossed the carpet to the bed. "Hey, everything okay?"

She pulled herself up on her elbows and nodded. "Yes."

"You sure? Because if someone slipped you another threatening note at the reception last night, for example, I would need to know."

She'd been so caught up in Cole, she'd all but forgotten the reason he'd come on this trip in the first place—to guard her. "No, it's nothing like that. I'm nervous about my presentation to the cabinet ministers this afternoon and worrying over what might be behind the Prime Minister's canceling." She caught herself raking her teeth over her bottom lip and stopped when she noticed the funny look on his face. Judging by the intensity of his eyes searching her face, his bullshit barometer must be on high alert.

"If you're sure that's all, I'll get going. The sooner I leave, the sooner I can get back." He dropped a kiss atop her head.

Eyeing his sexy backside as he walked toward the door, Alex sucked in a sigh. What an absolutely beautiful man, beautiful on the inside as well as the outside. Too bad he wasn't a keeper, only a rental.

Hand on the door, he turned back. "Two creams, no sugar, right?"

"You remember?" That she also remembered he took his strong and black was beside the point. Women tended to remember that sort of stuff, men less so.

His hand stalled on the rusted knob, shoulders bunching beneath the tight T-shirt. "I remember…everything. I'll be back as soon as I can. In the meantime, don't you so much as think about moving from this room. Got it?"

"Got it." She sent him a mock salute.

He opened the door and stepped out into the hall.

Alone once more, she slumped back against the pillows. After their incredible night and morning, she couldn't wait to have him again—so much for getting him out of her system. Being with him again had only increased her craving. It was the very reason she didn't keep chocolate in the house. As long as she stayed clear of temptation she was fine, but once she succumbed and took that first scrumptiously rich bite, she was a goner.

It didn't help that the chemistry was incredible, the sex hotter and more electric than she even remembered. Once they'd hit the sheets, there'd been no need to get reacquainted. But it was more than him knowing where to put his hands or her knowing just how to suck him. There was a sense of soul-deep connection, a transcendence that went beyond physical pleasure. She'd never before felt so close to another human being. They were amazing together, as amazing as she remembered, only better. Amazing in every way but one—she couldn't trust him not to hurt her again.

The previous experience had wrecked her emotionally. It had taken her a long time to pull together the pieces of her shattered heart and live again. She'd hit bottom and almost hadn't come back up. It wouldn't take much for her to fall in love with Cole all over again. She was more than halfway there. Could she sign up for risking heartbreak a second time?

Her job at Traxton involved not only developing and testing potential new products but also projecting whether the possible long-term payback justified the upfront investment and risk of going all the way to market. A quick-and-dirty cost-benefits analysis of her current situation confirmed what she already knew in her heart.

Falling in love with Cole again was a risk she couldn't afford to take.

ALEX STEPPED OUT of the shower and wrapped herself in the thin, scratchy bath towel. Coming back into the bedroom, she heard her cell phone beep, signaling a missed call and waiting message. Thinking it must be Cole calling to say he'd been held up, she dropped the towel and dialed her voice mail. Instead, the message was from Randall and apparently he'd left it last night.

"Call me." His voice held a sharp edge.

She speed-dialed him back, thinking of what she'd been doing last night in lieu of returning his call. The hand holding the phone began to shake.

He picked up on the third ring. "Randall, it's me."

"I was worried."

"I'm sorry I didn't call. It was a long travel day and an even longer night. There was a glitch with the limo and… Well, I don't want to bore you with all the details. It's all worked out."

"Are you sure? You don't sound like yourself."

She sighed. Apparently they were on track to have one of *those* conversations. "How do you mean?"

"Just now you sounded…very far away."

No doubt her guilty conscience was prompting her to nitpick for flaws, but regardless his clinginess grated. "I *am* far away, Randall, hundreds of miles, actually."

"You sound stressed. Do you perhaps need a valium?"

She drew a deep breath, wishing the air conditioning would kick in. "No, Randall, I don't need pharmaceuticals. What I need is to get to work. My presentation to the cabinet ministers is in a couple of hours. I'll call you afterward, okay?"

For once he didn't try to hold her up. "All right then, darling. Ciao."

Clicking off the call, she admitted she *was* stressed out, though that afternoon's presentation no longer topped her worry list. Occupying the number-one spot was Cole. He'd only been back in her life for a week, but already he'd managed to turn it upside down—again. They hadn't even been in Belize a full day, and already she'd done things she'd never imagined doing. Cheating on her fiancé with a contract employee who also happened to be the guy who'd once deserted her and broken her heart—what was she thinking? She wasn't thinking. That was the problem. Ever since they'd landed, she'd let rational thought take a backseat to emotion, and that approach had never led her anywhere that was good.

She was beginning to think the "smart bacteria" that had brought her to Belize might just be a hell of a lot smarter than she was.

DESPITE Alex's assurance she wasn't going anywhere, Cole didn't feel all that good about leaving her alone. As much as his ego might lead him to think that his sexual mojo had mellowed her out, he knew better. Alex was still Alex. She'd had a mind of her own five years ago, and she was even more stubborn now. Still, if he expected her to trust him with her safety and yes, her life, he'd better be prepared to return some of that trusting in kind. He really couldn't watch her 24/7. Sooner or later everyone had to sleep, use the bathroom, take a shower. Not that he would mind following her into the shower. If not for the pressing need to get a reliable rental car, he might be in there with her now.

The desk clerk from the day before greeted him, looking crisp and alert despite the already wilting heat. Cole explained his transportation problem, and, as he'd expected, the man was more than happy to help hook him up with a car. Though English-speaking and democratic, Belize wasn't really all that different from its Central American neighbors. Like most Third-World countries, barter was good, cash even better. As for the air conditioning, the clerk promised to send an engineer up within the hour. Having made headway on his two main goals, he saw about breakfast.

He returned to the suite with a cardboard tray of coffee and a modest sense of satisfaction. Alex was in her room. Wrapped in a towel, she sat on the side of the bed combing the tangles from her damp hair.

She looked up at him and smiled and, predictably, his heart did its Flipper routine. "That really was fast."

"I was really motivated."

He crossed the room. Dropping a kiss atop her head, he handed her a paper coffee cup from the tray along with a napkin-wrapped Belizean delicacy: the flaky, buttery flat biscuit known as a Johnny Cake. As far as calories and cholesterol went, the biscuits were absolutely deadly, addictively delicious. Then again, they were leaving on Friday morning, so there wouldn't be enough time for him to get hooked on much of anything—unless, of course, you counted Alex.

He took a sip of his coffee and sat down beside her. "I know you said you don't eat breakfast but I thought you might want to try a bite."

"Hmm, this is amazing." Watching her wolf down the biscuit, he hid a smile. For someone who swore she didn't eat breakfast, she polished off her pastry in record time.

Between bites, she asked, "Were you able to find a rental car already?"

He nodded. "The desk clerk's brother-in-law owns the rental car company, go figure. They're dropping off a four-wheel-drive SUV anytime now, which of course means at least another hour."

Laughing, she licked butter from her fingers. "Yep, after yesterday that sounds about right."

He cleared his throat. Feeling like a zit-faced kid about to launch into his first ask-out, he said, "So I was looking at the amended mission—I mean trip agenda—and I noticed that tomorrow is clear for you until the banquet and that's at night."

Blowing on her coffee, she said, "Well, there's nothing specific scheduled, if that's what you mean. I thought I'd just, you know, hang out here and work."

"But after your presentation today, isn't the rest of the trip more or less a waiting game until the cabinet vote comes in?"

She bristled and started playing with her coffee stir stick. "It is but… The Belize deal isn't the only project I'm working on."

He knew he probably shouldn't go there, but he couldn't help it. Reaching over, he lifted her chin and turned her face to look at him. "Don't you ever do anything just for fun?"

The question could have just as easily applied to him. These past five years he hadn't exactly been party central. Other than the occasional hike and the even more occasional skiing session, he pretty much worked nonstop.

But this wasn't about him. It was about Alex. When she didn't jump up and sling coffee at him, he pressed his advantage and put an arm about her shoulders. "You're in Belize, a country you've never been in before. Why not make the most of it? If you're going to be in Belize, then *see* Belize."

He stopped there, thinking that coffee might be coming his way sooner rather than later. Instead she turned her head to him and said, "You know, you're right."

Cole was so surprised he almost fell off the bed. "You're kidding, right?"

She shook her head, decisive, utterly resolute. "Nope, I really think you have a point, Whittaker. I need to get out more. Just to be clear, though, did you just ask me out on a date?"

"I was thinking of it as more of, you know, an outing."

"An outing, that's interesting." She went back to sipping her coffee.

"Why do you ask?"

She shrugged, this time without looking up. "No special reason."

Meaning there was at least one not-so-special reason. "Do you want me to ask you out on a date?" Watching her profile for clues, he added, "Because, you know, if you wanted that, I could."

She shrugged. "Date, outing—like they say, a rose by any other name... Only since you made the suggestion, the onus is on you to organize whatever it is you think I shouldn't leave Belize without experiencing."

Cole's heart leapfrogged. She'd just agreed to spend the better part of tomorrow with him...anywhere he wanted to take her...just the two of them...alone!

"How does adventure sound?"

"It sounds perfect." She turned and smiled at him, not only with her sexy full mouth but also with her eyes. "The only caveat—okay, *rule*—is that you also have to get me back to the hotel in plenty of time to make the banquet. And by the way, plenty of time means at least an hour."

He held out his hand. "Deal."

National Assembly, Later that Day

ALEX LOOKED UP from the lectern out to the auditorium of Belizean cabinet ministers, representatives, senators and associated staffers, the glasses she used for reading riding low on her nose. "And in conclusion, the Traxton Biotech approach to bacterial bioremediation will not only revolutionize petroleum clean-up globally but also open the door to new eco-friendly development opportunities for Belize for decades to come."

She stepped back from the podium amidst a shower of applause. Her presentation, complete with slides, was an obvious hit. Projected on the roll-down screen behind her was a blow-up of the smart bacteria, the many microbes forming an elegant, dragon-like tail.

She caught Phillip Collins's stony gaze from one of the middle rows and felt a flash of defiance. His presentation, which had preceded hers, had been full of techno-flash, but to anyone with a microbiology background, the system he proposed had more holes than...well, than the sinkhole. His grim expression, not so smug now, confirmed her presentation really had gone off well. Let him write whatever threatening note he pleased. It was too late now.

Afterward she received compliments from the cabinet ministers and legislative staffers. The Prime Minister, a distinguished dark-skinned Creole in his sixties, walked up and shook her hand.

"That was a most thorough treatment of the topic, Miss Kendall. Your firm is fortunate to have you. I particularly appreciate the eco-friendly measures you propose for mining the bacteria."

Alex acknowledged the compliment with a nod. Ensuring that the sinkhole site remained intact was something she'd fought for from the beginning. The careful mining techniques would incur greater upfront costs, but in the end the blue hole would be preserved to be enjoyed by generations of divers. Not everything was about the bottom line, or at least it shouldn't be.

"My main concern when Western companies come in is that oftentimes things set forth on paper are not always brought into reality once the agreement is made. I would not like to think Traxton Biotech was such a firm."

Alex understood what he was asking. "You have my word that should Traxton Biotech be awarded the contract, we will honor its terms to the letter."

"You will be overseeing the project personally, then?"

Alex hesitated. She was so close to closing the deal, she could almost taste the Veuve Clicquot on her tongue, and yet her personal policy was to never lie. "I had planned to resign once I married, but now it seems I'll be staying on." Assuming Randall didn't fire her, that is. "Either way, I will make sure that whoever works on phase one of the project shares our philosophy and mission."

He stared at her, expression inscrutable, and Alex wondered if her honesty-is-the-best-policy credo had just blown more than six months of work.

Finally he spoke. "I will see you at the banquet tomorrow evening. Until then, Miss Kendall, I hope you enjoy your time in Belize. Have you had the opportunity to see much beyond the capital?"

Glad that honesty couldn't possibly get her into trouble on this front at least, she eagerly answered, "I have plans to do some sightseeing tomorrow."

"That is good, very good. To understand Belize, first you must experience her with all your senses." He backed away with a bow.

As she watched him walk out, it occurred to her that Cole had said much the same thing.

DRESSED in a lightweight dark suit and tie, Cole waited for her in the corridor outside. "How did it go?"

"I think I may have blown the deal but other than that, swell."

He looked surprised. "Your presentation didn't go well?"

She shook her head. "The presentation went great. I know this sounds pompous, but I blew Phil and Sun Coast out of the water."

"So what's the problem?"

Alex hesitated. Honesty might be the best policy, or at least her policy, but that didn't mean she was obliged to blab every little detail, especially when doing so might cause her to run the very real risk of looking like a dope—and getting hurt again. Normal people didn't change their lives for a fling. That morning she'd told herself she'd be calling things off with Randall, but now it struck her that everything might look very different once she got back to New York. As bad as she felt about cheating, technically she wasn't married to Randall yet or living with him, for that matter. If she did go through with the wedding, she would be a good and faithful wife. Lots of people probably had final flings before they tied the knot. Fling, who was she kidding? Cole would always mean more to her than a casual lover no matter how many bargains she made with herself. Still, she didn't have to decide this moment or even today.

"On second thought, I'm probably overreacting."

Expression amused, he gestured a hand toward her face. "When did you start wearing glasses?"

She'd been so wigged out after her talk with the Prime Minister she'd forgotten to take them off. Self-conscious, she touched the side of the wire frame. "About a year ago, I guess. They're only for reading," she added, not wanting to seem old.

"You look cute in them."

"Cute, huh?" As compliments came, "cute" had never topped her list of favorites.

"Well, okay, maybe *cute* isn't exactly the right word. You've got sort of a sexy-librarian thing going on."

Sexy librarian was definitely a step up from cute. "Don't tell me, let me guess. You had a lot of overdue library books as a kid?"

He didn't deny it. Arms folded behind his back, he looked around the hallway. Seeing they were more or less alone, he leaned in and whispered, "Wear them for me later…in bed."

"Anything else you want me to wear?"

A grin split his handsome face from ear to ear. "Not a damned thing."

10

Thursday, Day Three

THE NEXT MORNING Alex stood with Cole in the pull-up outside their hotel waiting for the valet to bring the rental car around. Dressed in a white polo shirt and jeans, he glanced down at her feet. "Those shoes have definitely got to go." He still hadn't let on where he was taking her, though his comment suggested walking would be involved.

Her footwear wasn't the only thing requiring a redo. Her pale-yellow linen sheath dress was perfect for a summer stroll in Manhattan, but in this sultry, colorful country, it seemed out of place. Since they'd arrived, she'd taken note of what the local women wore—bright sarong-style dresses, peasant blouses paired with bold floral-print skirts and strappy sandals.

"I only brought work clothes and evening wear. I guess I didn't count on doing much—any—sightseeing." She'd packed her running shoes and some Spandex gym wear but those would be too casual. "I'm going to need to buy some play clothes." At her mention of shopping, he looked surprised but not particularly put out as so many men might. Not wanting to come off like one of "those women," she rushed to reassure him. "I promise it won't take long."

He reached for her hand, long, thick fingers lacing hers.

"Hey, as long as buying new stuff involves you taking off the old stuff first, take as long as you like. Fortunately it's a market day. Let's go see what they've got."

Holding hands, they walked toward the market square. The temperature had cooled slightly from the previous night's rain. No doubt it would be stifling as the day wore on, but for now a pleasant breeze stirred the air.

Casting Cole a sideways glance, Alex felt as if Manhattan and Randall were worlds rather than mere miles away. So far Cole had given her no indication he intended to continue seeing her once they got back to the States. Unlike her, he seemed to have no problem sticking to their bargain. Regardless, being with him like this brought home everything she'd missed these past five years. Signing up for a modern-day marriage of convenience no longer seemed like the practical solution she'd talked herself into believing it could be. Warty frogs and false princes aside, settling for less than true love just seemed empty and sad.

But for the moment she was in an exotic fairy-tale land strolling hand-in-hand with the man she'd once thought of as her personal Prince Charming. Fretting over the future would only spoil what little time they had left.

Reaching the square, they climbed the few steps to the sun-baked stones. On their arrival the other day, Belmopan had seemed a sleepy little town, but market day presented a very different atmosphere. Aisles of vendor stalls greeted them, displaying an array of goods from local produce and plants, hand-crafted baskets and furniture, to a mouthwatering array of prepared hot and cold foods, including the popular local dishes, beans-and-rice and rice-and-beans. Cole explained that in the first dish, the beans were cooked separately and then spooned with their gravy over white rice; in the latter, the ingredients were mixed together stew-fashion in a single pot. Who knew! Women carrying market baskets and wearing wide-brimmed straw hats pushed past. Pockets of people, including a few obvious tourists, congregated around the Creole folk band playing from the one palm tree-shaded corner. Alex could almost believe she was back in Manhattan browsing the green market in Union Square and the frequent street fairs held elsewhere in Greenwich Village. Walking through, she made a mental note to pick up not only a hat but sunglasses as well. The light striking the white granite was almost blinding. Eyes watering, she spotted a stall selling brightly colored cotton clothing.

She tugged on Cole's arm, signaling for them to stop. Rummaging through the racks, she quickly picked out a white cotton peasant-style blouse and a brightly colored flounced skirt.

She turned to him. "I'll be right back."

"If you need a fashion consultant, you know where to find me."

He followed up the offer with a grin, the broad smile bringing out the crinkle lines at the corners of his eyes. Maybe the sun was playing tricks on her, but it seemed that since coming to Belize the color of his eyes had deepened.

As she met his gaze, her heart lurched. Tomorrow was Friday, their final day together, but most of it would be spent traveling. With Randall's flight crew, Kim especially, catering to their every need, they'd have no real privacy. Practically speaking their fairy-tale fling ended not at the stroke of midnight but once the alarm went off in the morning. It was a depressing thought.

She tried covering her sadness with a smile. "Thanks, I'll keep it in mind."

Garments draped over her arm, she pulled aside the worn

curtain and slipped inside the makeshift tent. The close air was heavy with the scents of dye and raw cotton, the heat intense. Stepping out of the heavy, lined linen dress was a relief. Facing herself in the rust-spotted dressing mirror, she slipped on the cool cotton garments, instantly feeling not only lighter but freer, too. She pulled the clip from her hair, and shook it out, running a hand through the tousled waves. Wow. No one would mistake her for a local but she certainly looked…different, carefree and young and yes, just a little bit reckless. Casting a critical eye on her reflection, she decided the outfit could probably use a chunky necklace and a pair of funky, dangling earrings, the sort of artsy stuff she used to wear but which had lain fallow at the bottom of her jewelry box for years. There were several jewelry artisans who'd set up shop in the square, but she didn't want to spend any more of her and Cole's precious outing shopping. Until now she hadn't realized how very much she was looking forward to being outside the city and alone with him.

She turned to go when a wicked impulse had her whipping back around. If she was going to be reckless and carefree for the day, why not give it her one-hundred-percent personal-best effort? Heart pounding, she turned back to the mirror. Her eyes looked more a rich chicory than her usual honey-brown, her naked lips kiss-swollen and berry-red, her hair a crazy curly mess that, she had to admit, suited her. She scarcely recognized herself and that, she decided, was a very good thing. Watching her face in the mirror, she slipped a hand beneath her skirt and pulled her panties down and then off. Grinning, she looked down. The little cream-colored thong pooled at her feet. Thick, heavy air funneled beneath her skirt. The space between her thighs was slightly sore from two days of Cole's loving and deliciously damp, so much so that she found herself regretting not taking him up on his offer to come inside with her. A quickie in public and yet hidden from view would have been the perfect launch to their afternoon's adventure. Then again, they had the whole afternoon ahead of them. Whatever he had planned, she'd be surprised if making love wasn't a prominent part of it. She scooped up the panties and tucked them inside her bag.

Pulling the flap back, she stepped out into the blinding brightness. Something about standing out in the open in full daylight brought her inhibitions back in a rush. God, had she really just done that, taken off her underwear? The warm air funneling beneath her skirt assured her she had, but there was no turning back now. Self-conscious, she stole a glance at Cole, suddenly feeling very much like her shy former self.

Refusing to be that girl again, she forced her gaze up to his and held her arms out from her sides. "You like?"

The heat burning in his blue eyes confirmed he did, very much so. "You're beautiful." His gaze slid over her, settling on the shadow of cleavage left bare by the blouse's scooped neckline. "Damn." Shaking his head, he turned toward the vendor and reached inside his pocket.

Caught up in the magic of the moment, Alex took several seconds before she realized what he was about to do. She shot out a hand, fingers wrapping around his wrist. "You put that money back where it came from, mister." Seeing him clench his jaw, noting the vendor watching them closely, she dropped her voice to a whisper. "Cole, please, I can't let you buy me clothes."

Clothing was altogether too personal a gift to accept from a man with whom she was having just a fling, a man whom in all likelihood she wouldn't be seeing again after tomorrow. Long-term lovers and married couples bought clothes for each other. Fuck buddies sprung for sex toys and beers.

His gaze skimmed her face and then he looked sharply away. "Then don't think of it as clothes. Think of it as a souvenir of our trip, and by the way, I'm not taking no for an answer."

She could argue with him, she *should* argue with him, but she couldn't bring herself to spoil either the moment or the day.

Swallowing against the sudden lump blocking her throat, she accepted with a nod. "In that case, thank you."

"In that case, you're welcome."

He turned away to pay, and Alex took the opportunity to blink the tears from her eyes. Everybody knew that a "souvenir" was the forerunner to goodbye.

THEY TURNED onto the scenic Hummingbird Highway and headed east toward the coast, the Maya mountains a continuous, gently rolling slope. Cole still hadn't told her their destination, although as they drove on, the roadside signage for various state parks and attractions narrowed down the range of possibilities. Not that it mattered to Alex. As long as she was alone with Cole, blissfully and thoroughly alone, she was happy to take part in whatever adventure he had in mind.

They'd been in the car for about an hour when he pulled onto the shoulder of the road beneath what remained of an old railway bridge. Switching off the engine, he turned to her. "There's someplace I want to take you, but we're going to have to go the rest of the way on foot."

Before leaving the market square, she'd traded in her Manolo sling backs for a pair of Birkenstock sandals, which they'd picked up at a cleverly converted shipping container turned shoe store located on the market edge. Now she was very glad she had.

They parked and got out of the car, Cole coming around to her side. "Where are we, by the way?"

Taking her hand, he grinned. "If I tell you, it won't be a surprise."

They were in a tropical forest, very probably a nature preserve or national park, though they hadn't gone through any admission gate. Holding on to her, he led her down a steep slope. The sounds of splashing and the scent of limestone grew more pronounced as they went deeper in.

It took about fifteen minutes before they reached bottom, the trail dead-ending. Cole let go of her, stepped ahead, and swept aside an overhang of vines. Holding the curtain of foliage aside, he beckoned for her to go through. She did. Stepping out on the other side, she caught her breath. A tropical Garden of Eden spread out before her, a waterfall dominating the scene. The falls emptied into a lagoon, the water an intense sapphire-blue and banked by lush greenery and brightly colored flowers.

Alex took a deep breath of the thick, fragrant air and turned around to Cole. "It's perfect. Now I feel like I've seen Belize. Thank you."

He beamed at her. "I discovered this place while hiking seven years ago. After my mission ended, I tacked on a week to stay and explore. I haven't been back since."

"Off the beaten path" didn't begin to describe just how alone they seemed to be. She doubted the location was marked on any tourist map, at least not the kind marketed to Americans.

Cole was lifting his shirt over his head. He shucked off the shirt and tossed it on a boulder. Her gaze fixed on his bare chest, dappled by shade and kissed by sunshine, and she sucked in her breath, suddenly feeling as if she was drowning in the moist air.

He rolled down the zipper of his jeans. She swallowed hard, wishing she'd thought to bring the bottle of water she'd left back at the car. "What, uh…are you doing?"

He stepped out of the jeans and turned to toss them onto the rock, where they joined his shirt. "I'd think that would be pretty obvious. I'm going for a swim. C'mon and join me." He held out his hand to her.

Alex stayed rooted to the rocks. He wasn't wearing briefs, and though she'd been to bed with him any number of times, the sight of him standing fully, gloriously naked and semi-erect in broad daylight caught her off guard. He was the perfect modern-day Adam, all wide shoulders and tapered waist, powerful thighs and firm ass. The latter made her mouth water and she experienced a strong urge to walk over, bend down and take a bite of forbidden fruit. She didn't dare.

He climbed over the rim of rocks and lowered himself into the water. Up close it looked more crystalline than blue. He dove under and then reemerged, water plastering his hair to his head and sluicing his broad shoulders, droplets dribbling down his lean torso, drawing Alex's eye to the queue of dark hair leading below the water's edge.

Breathe, Alex, just breathe.

Watching him, she was aware that her skin felt feverish and hypersensitive, the points of her nipples poking through the thin blouse, the light cotton skirt suddenly far too heavy, like a millstone weighing her down.

Cole tunneled his hand through his hair and called out, "It's like bathwater. Come on in." He swam up to the edge of the rocks and stretched out a sinewy arm.

She stayed put and shook her head. The closest she'd ever come to having sex out in the open had been one time with Cole five years ago when they'd taken advantage of an un-seasonally mild night to go camping. But making love in a sleeping bag and at night was a far cry from what he seemed to be suggesting.

Dousing himself again, he let out a snort. "I've seen every gorgeous inch of you up close and personal—and done a hell of a lot more than just looked."

"I'm not worried about you seeing me."

That statement fell between a half truth and an outright lie. Despite her heavy schedule, she found time to work out, including long runs on the Hudson River Park several times a week. Still, thirty-five wasn't twenty-five or even thirty. Her breasts were fuller than they used to be, but they also weren't quite as firm. Fortunately she'd been blessed with a trim waistline and narrow hips, but lately she'd noticed that her butt seemed to be listing ever so slightly south. Direct sunlight was pretty unforgiving. She wasn't so sure she was ready to let it all hang out with him.

Cole, on the other hand, was perfect.

"Then what?" The knowing look on his face told her his bullshit barometer must be going off big-time.

She shrugged, aware that her clothing had begun to cling to her damp skin. "I'm just not all that interested in flashing passersby. Giving some little kid on vacation with his family his first anatomy lesson isn't high on my list."

Fingers raking the water, he rolled his eyes. "It's November. The kids are in school here, too. Besides, technically speaking, you've never really undressed for me. Consider this me putting in a request."

Breathe, Alex, just breathe.

He swam over to the shallow edge where his feet touched bottom and stood. Water lapped at his bare skin, plastering the dark hair to his arms, chest and legs. Now that he was more than halfway out of the water, she no longer had to imagine where the dark line trailing down his abdomen led. The water must be warm indeed because his semi had throttled to a full-on erection. The sight of him, long and thick and hard, raised a keen, pulsing ache. Suddenly, getting naked seemed not so much an occasion for embarrassment as a task that would take entirely too much time.

She started toward him, but he shook his head. "I want you naked, Alex. I want you to come to me as bare as the day you were born."

Alex hesitated. After tomorrow, she wouldn't be seeing him again. This was their last day together in Belize. Why not make it memorable?

She pulled the peasant blouse over her head and dropped it on the dry area of rocks. Next, she kicked off her sandals. Knowing that his eyes followed her every move, she forced herself to slow down.

Breathe Alex, just breathe.

Her skirt she saved for last. She stepped out of it, and Cole's jaw dropped. "All this time you've been riding around without underwear?"

She cleared her throat. "I took them off when I went inside the tent to change."

His stark gaze struck hers. "Do you have any idea how turned-on that makes me?"

Taking in the turgid flesh standing out from his thighs, she answered, "I think I have a pretty good idea."

His eyes, not icy now but the same warm inviting blue of the lagoon, held hers. "In that case, no more stalling. Come here, you." He held out his hand.

And in that instant Alex gave up on worrying about the firmness of her breasts and the tightness of her tush. This time she didn't hesitate. She took Cole's hand, stepped over the rocks, and walked into the water. He hadn't lied. She'd braced herself for cold, but the temperature was amazing, like bathwater. He guided her deeper, until it reached her neck.

Treading water, she looked deeply into his eyes. "This may sound corny, but now that we're here, I have to admit one of my fantasies has always been to make love beneath a waterfall."

She didn't have to say more than that. Side by side they swam the yard or so to the falls. They neared the cascade, and warm water churned about them, the friction playing with the sensitive place between Alex's legs. Ordinarily she would have been afraid of being pulled down by the current, but she was with Cole, and she knew she could entrust her physical safety to him, if not her heart. When he took her hand to lead her underwater, she didn't hesitate. She held her breath, closed her eyes, and dunked. When they emerged, they were on the other side of the screen of cascading water.

He lifted her hand to his mouth and kissed her fingertips. "Happy?"

Beneath the water, her hands found his hips. His flesh beneath her fingers felt cool and smooth, the muscles rippling not unlike the water. "Do you even have to ask?"

It occurred to her they'd had a similar conversation five years ago but that suddenly seemed a lifetime ago, the past. She lifted one hand and slid her fingers into his sluiced-back hair. Surrounded on all sides by paradise, she felt like Eve to his Adam, possessive, primal.

Looking up into his eyes, she said, "I want you," and in her heart that didn't mean for the day or even another four, but forever.

"You have me. You've always had me." He slid his hands to her waist and pulled her close, close enough that she could feel his hardness pressing into her lower belly. "I didn't want to leave you at the airport."

"I know you didn't." And amazingly, she did.

Throat working, he laid his forehead along hers. "I swore to myself that after the mission wrapped, I'd find you and tell you everything about who I was, my job, all of it. Afterward, assuming you stuck around instead of kicking me to the curb, I'd ask you to marry me."

"You wanted to marry me?" Her gasp broke through the rushing water.

He drew back, seeming surprised that this was news to her. "I'd even picked out a ring."

If only she could go back in time, she'd set aside her stubborn pride and take his calls. Unfortunately she'd listened to her mother, given in to her insecurities, and been all too quick to assume he was a player.

Swallowing hard, she admitted, "I would have married you in a heartbeat."

"What you said the other day, you were right. I could have broken protocol and called you with some bullshit excuse. Even a text message saying something had come up, an emergency, would have been enough. I would have caught hell for it and gotten written up for it later, but I had enough points racked up to weather whatever punishment they dished out."

"Then why didn't you?" She wasn't so sure she really wanted to hear his answer, but at least he was talking now and she was listening and the opportunity was altogether too precious to pass up. Beyond that, she simply needed to know.

He swallowed hard, the ripple traveling the corded tendons of his throat. "Looking back on it all now, I think I must have been testing you, seeing if you had what it takes to be the wife of an HRT operative. It's not an easy life by any means, and God knows I was too damned arrogant to consider giving it up."

"I see."

He shook his head and for a moment she wondered if he had water in his ears, then she realized he must be trying to shake any cloudiness from his head. This was the most honesty they'd shared in…well, ever.

"I think I wasn't testing you as much as myself. Before we met, the team, the job were damned near everything to me. And then suddenly I found myself living for the weekends because that was when I got to see you. On some level, I think I was afraid that things working out between us would mean my losing my edge…me."

"So you thought you'd see how hard you could push before you pushed me away?"

He hesitated and then nodded. "Yeah, I guess so. Pretty fucked-up, I know."

"Yes, it is, but no more than me blocking your e-mail address and refusing your phone calls."

"I guess we both screwed up."

"Yeah, I guess we did."

For the first time ever, she felt not only completely turned on, but also completely at peace. Leaning forward, she brushed her mouth over his. His lips felt cool and firm. She slid her hand lower, her palm and fingertips registering the ripples of his washboard belly and then the coarse curls and turgid flesh beneath.

Breathe Alex, just breathe.

She drew a deep breath, held it, and dove beneath the water. Opening her eyes, she reached out and slid him into her mouth. Suckling for those precious thirty seconds or so, feeling him thrust into her mouth even as his hand reached beneath the water to cradle the back of her head, she told herself she had him. She really had him.

But for how long?

AFTERWARD, they dried off as best they could, then dressed and hiked up to where they'd left the car. They still hadn't had lunch. As fulfilling as the sex had been, the emotional revelations had all but wrecked Cole. He hadn't felt so mentally and physically drained since his HRT training concluded. Eating wasn't high on his present priority list, but there was Alex to consider. He'd promised her lunch and he was done with breaking his promises to her, even the small ones. Beyond that, he didn't want her to arrive at the banquet that night with an empty stomach and a light head.

But the clock was ticking. He'd promised to deliver her back to the hotel with an hour's lead time at least, which meant forgoing the charming cliffside inn he'd planned on taking her to. Fortunately there were a few decent restaurants within Belmopan. Once they got back into town, they could grab a late lunch and still have plenty of time to get ready for the banquet.

Keeping one eye on the narrow ribbon of roadway, he glanced over at Alex. Her eyes were drifting closed. She must be halfway to sleep, maybe more than halfway. Damp curls framed her face, making her look almost like a little girl. Her mouth was once more swollen from his kisses, her cheeks rosy from the sun and the grazing of his beginning beard.

The skidding of tires had him snapping his attention to his rearview mirror. *What the fuck...*

The white Bronco barreled down the narrow ribbon of roadway toward them and plastered itself to his bumper, the driver making no attempt to pass. Cole shot a quick look into his rearview mirror, but the driver wore sunglasses and a hat and sat hunkered behind the wheel. Seconds later, the Bronco rammed them in the rear, hard enough to throw them across the yellow dividing line, the skull-rattling jolt making him glad he always insisted on safety belts.

Alex came awake with a small scream.

Keeping his eyes on the road, he shouted, "Hold on, Lex," and swung out with his right arm, lashing her to the seat.

This wasn't a case of a drunk on the road or a randomly aggressive driver. Whoever was behind the wheel of the Bronco fully intended to run them off the road, maybe even send them over the guardrail to the cliff bottom. Fortunately high-speed evasive driving was an area of particular expertise.

Cole silently counted to five and then swerved to the left. The tail obviously hadn't anticipated that. The Bronco skidded, its left side smashing into the guardrail. Cole floored the gas, and they shot away.

Alex sat upright. "What was…that?" She ran a shaking hand through her tangled, still-damp hair.

Cole swallowed a deep breath and peeled his damp back from the seat. "I think we just got a crash course, so to speak, in Belizean driving."

He cast a sideways glance her way and caught her rolling her eyes. "I'm not that gullible, at least not anymore. Spill it."

"Okay, I'd say that was someone's best effort to make sure you were a no-show at tonight's banquet."

Predictably, her shoulders slumped and her face fell. Gnawing at her lower lip, she admitted, "I'd almost convinced myself the note was a hoax, but suddenly this whole death-threat thing is getting a little too real."

Wishing he could do more to comfort her, he settled for reaching across the seat and laying a hand on her shoulder. "For what it's worth, I think they mainly were trying to scare us—you. Still, I'd be very interested to know how and where our buddy Phil spent his afternoon. For his sake, he'd better have one hell of an airtight alibi."

11

THERE WAS something about surviving a near-death experience that brought out a person's thirst. If Cole had been alone when the incident happened, he would have shrugged it off in the first five minutes. But he hadn't been alone. He'd had Alex with him in the car.

Though obviously shaken, she was once again a total trouper. The one time he'd ventured to suggest she might want to cancel her appearance at the banquet, she'd gone ballistic, swearing she wasn't going to cave in to the cowardice of a weak-chinned bully like Phillip Collins or whoever had driven that car. Cole tried to convince her to reconsider, but secretly he was proud of her.

As soon as he drove into the hotel pull-up, she announced, "I don't want to come off like a lush, but I could really use a beer."

Cole flipped his keys to the valet, got out and rounded the car to her side. Opening the passenger-side door, he said, "Given what you've just been through, I'll hold off on staging any interventions. I could use one myself. How about I go into the bar and get us a couple of cold ones and whatever you want to eat to take up to the room?"

Stepping out, she flashed him a look of gratitude. "That would be so great. Thank you."

"The catch is you have to come with me." Odds were the bozo

who'd tried turning them into road kill was still stranded, but the episode had underscored this wasn't the time or place to take chances. Until they boarded the jet tomorrow, Alex was a target.

She nodded. "I need to use the restroom anyway. You know, splash some cold water on my face—at least I'm hoping it comes out of the pipes cold."

They entered through the automatic doors and cut across the lobby. The lounge didn't reopen until five, but fortunately the poolside bar was open and doing a brisk business. They threaded through the swimsuit-clad crowd, Alex breaking off toward the bathrooms. Keeping one eye on the ladies' room door, Cole walked over to the bar.

Catching the bartender's eye, he called out, "Two beers, whatever you have cold and in a bottle."

The bartender uncapped two bottles of a local brew and slid them across the bar. Cole had one hand on his money clip when a voice he'd hoped never to hear again called out, "Well, if it isn't Special Agent Whittaker."

He swung around to see Tony Sumatra sidling over, his gut poking out from a Hawaiian-style shirt so shiny it had to be polyester, the tropical sun glancing off the top of his mostly bald, bullet-shaped head. Tony's given name was Roger but his resemblance to James Gandolfini, the actor who'd played Tony Soprano, had caused the nickname to stick.

Well, wasn't this turning out to be a peach of a day? First Alex and he almost wound up at the bottom of a cliff and now it was shaping up to be old-home week with his buddy, Tony, who he'd helped to put away seven years ago.

Leaning back against the bar, Cole pulled back on his beer, taking his time before answering, "What brings you to Belize, Tony? No, don't tell me, let me guess. Drug-trafficking, weapons-smuggling, or maybe you have a new game these days? I mean, why stick to same old, same old when there's a smorgasbord of great crimes just waiting to be committed?" Arguably he was being an asshole, but guys like Tony didn't come to Central America just to get a tan.

Tony smirked. "You might say I'm celebrating Independence Day."

As good as a cold beer tasted on a hot day, Cole wished he and Alex had gone straight up to the room. Now the best he could hope was that Tony would beat it before she got back.

"Congratulations, how long you been out?"

Tony lifted his thick shoulders in a shrug. "Coupla weeks."

Cole mentally calculated the odds that he and Tony just happened to be in Belize at the same time, and though he supposed it was possible, most things were, he didn't see it as likely. Tony had a rap sheet as long as Cole's arm and a very personal reason for hating him.

"I thought I'd take the old lady on a little vacation, you know, show her my appreciation for waiting for me all these years—well, sorta waiting."

"That's nice, Tony, real romantic. I didn't know you were such a family man." Cole looked around, trying to picture the woman who would cast in her lot with a loser like Tony. "Where is she?"

Tony hesitated. "She's upstairs resting up for tonight if you know what I mean." He drove the point home with an elbow jab to Cole's ribs.

Cole glanced at the con's empty beer can, willing him to order his next one and walk away before Alex got back. But it seemed luck wasn't on his side, not today at least.

"That your woman?" Tony jerked his wobbly chins toward the back of the bar. Without turning around, Cole knew what or rather who he must be seeing. Alex, beautiful, brave, already shaken up Alex, who'd be stepping out of the ladies' room about now and making her way toward them.

Cole tensed, on instant alert, but he willed his breathing to steady and his features to fall into a nonchalant mask. "I don't see as that's any of your business, but I appreciate the interest."

Alex picked that moment to throw her arm up in the air and wave, her peasant blouse sliding off one sunburned shoulder. Tony's low catcall set Cole's teeth on edge. "She's a real looker, ladylike…expensive."

Cole fisted his hand on the beer bottle, doing his damn best to forestall fantasies of how good it would feel to break it over the felon's head. To scum like Tony, everything and everyone was a commodity to be bought, sold, or better yet, stolen. "She's not for sale."

Tony's Jack o' lantern grin confirmed he'd just exposed himself in a major way. "I didn't say she was. I was just thinking, you know, out loud."

"Well, do your thinking somewhere else," Cole snapped, and slammed a Belizean twenty down on the bar. "Have another couple on me—somewhere else." So much for playing it cool.

Tony scowled, at the same time sweeping up the money with hands the size of small hams. "Hey, you might have sent me away seven years ago, but I done my time. I'm a free man now, free to come and go as I please." Tony's mouth took on an ugly twist. "You're the one who'd better watch his back, *Special Agent* Whittaker. On second thought, you're not so special anymore. Popped any kids lately?"

It seemed incarceration in the state pen didn't necessarily mean you were out of the loop. Cole opened his mouth to answer when Alex walked up beside him. "Sorry I took so long. There was a line." She turned to Tony. "Hello."

"Hel-lo, gorgeous." Tony gave her the once-over, a slow, up-and-down perusal calculated to drive Cole crazy, which it did. "Have my seat, I was just leaving." He flashed a broken-toothed smile and patted the vinyl-covered cushion.

"Thank you." She took the stool and Cole resisted the urge to grab a fistful of bar napkins and wipe it off first. Slime balls like Tony tended to stick to whatever and whomever they touched.

She glanced at Cole's half-finished beer and then to the full one still sitting on the bar. "I'm really hoping that one's got my name on it."

It took him several seconds for the broad hint to sink in. "Sorry, you bet it is." He handed her the beer, ashamed at having let a loser like Tony get to him.

"Thanks." She put the bottle to her lips and tilted it back, taking a healthy swallow. "Hmm, that's good, whatever it is. Who was that?" she asked.

"Who was who?"

She looked up and rolled her eyes. "The heavyset balding man you were just talking with. He looks kind of like Tony Soprano, don't you think?"

Cole hesitated. She had enough on her plate without worrying about criminals, *former* criminals, roaming the resort. Besides, under the U.S. justice system, people were innocent until proven guilty, even ex-cons. Despite his tough talking, Tony really might be here on vacation with his wife. Stranger things had happened. Sure, right. And while he was at it, there might really be an Easter Bunny and a Santa Claus, too.

Cole shrugged. "Just another hotel guest." Strictly speaking, it was the truth. "You want something to eat? If you'd rather, we can get something to take back to the room. Or I can order room service while you're getting ready."

She shook her head. "Thanks, but it turns out I'm not so hungry."

He made a point of glancing at his watch. "Well, it is getting late. We'd better get you upstairs."

Not giving her an opportunity to answer, he picked up her beer, hooked an arm about her shoulders and shuttled her toward the lobby.

She cast him a sideways stare. "If I didn't know better, I'd think you were trying to get me out of the way."

A middle-aged woman with a perma tan and a floppy-brimmed sunhat bumped into him, saving him from answering. Shoving a shaking hand of fang-like red fingernails into her straw beach bag, she shot up her bleached-blond head.

"Sorry, my bad." She flashed him a yellow smoker's smile and held up the cigarette pack she'd just fished out. "Gotta have my ciggies, ya know."

Glad he'd never taken up the habit, Cole nodded, wondering why his scalp prickled. Sunburn, maybe? "No problem." He and Alex continued on to the elevators. The doors opened, and he motioned for Alex to step on the elevator in front of him.

The doors closed and she turned to him. "Is there something you're not telling me? If there is, give it up."

He shrugged. "You made me promise not to make you late. Not being late for stuff seems to be a really big deal for you. The way I see it, I'm just holding up my end of our deal."

Too bad the deal closed after tomorrow.

"How IS the mission proceeding?" Beethoven asked.

The static over the line and the blaring of beach music in the background made it hard to hear, but he thought Tony's answer came across as "Not so good."

He clamped one hand over the desk's edge. "Elaborate."

Tony cleared his throat. "Whittaker must have been a NASCAR driver in a previous life. Irma lost her nerve and ended up crashing the Bronco into the guardrail."

"You let your wife drive!" Beethoven choked on the sip of Glenlivet he'd just taken.

"We're a team, Irma and me, and well, since I got hit on the head with the crowbar that last time in, I don't see so good. I tried again once they got back to the hotel, but Whittaker stuck to her like glue. He rushed her up to the room before I had a chance. Jesus, you'd think after fucking her all day he'd give it a rest. If his bodyguarding business doesn't work out, he's a shoo-in for them Viagra commercials."

Beethoven prided himself on expecting the unexpected and planning accordingly, but he hadn't come close to expecting…this. "Excuse me?"

"Broad's got some libido on her, that's for sure. She's been getting busy with her bodyguard ever since they stepped off the jet."

"You're certain of this?"

"A picture says a thousand words, and Irma's telephoto lens don't lie. The Kendall broad sure is photogenic. Before today, who would have guessed all that va-va-voom was beneath them buttoned-up suits?" He let out a low whistle.

Beethoven had little interest in hearing the unsavory details. He sank back in his seat and rubbed two fingers over the pounding in his temples, willing plan B to take shape in his mind.

Alex had done her job well, too well. According to his mole in the Belizean ministry, Biotech would be announced as the contract award recipient at the banquet that night. It was vitally important that she not be there to accept. Her absence would be perceived as an unpardonable sin, a slap in the face to the Belizean government and people. By default, the Belizean ministry would award the contract to Sun Coast.

Snapping upright, he said, "If you can't keep Alex Kendall from arriving at the banquet, then make certain she disappears tonight before the contract award is announced."

"Okay, but how?"

He bit back a curse. Tony was the classic example of all brawn and no brains. In their blessedly brief association, he'd more than disproved the popular belief that all career criminals were masterminds.

"If Cole Whittaker is her weakness, then use it—*him*—against her."

THE NOTES to Beethoven's Fifth rang out from inside Alex's purse as she and Cole came up to her hotel-room door. The symphony was Randall's favorite, hence her programming it into her phone as his signature ring tone. He played the CD nonstop in the car, the office, you name it.

Avoiding meeting Cole's eye, she fumbled in her purse and fished out the cell, dribbling beer onto the carpet. Silently, he took the key from her and slipped it into the slotted lock, pushed the door open and stepped back.

"My darling, how are you? I couldn't reach you, I was growing worried."

Cradling the phone in the crook of her neck and shoulder, she stepped inside and headed for her bedroom. "Hi, yes, well, cell phone reception's not so great here. I'm just getting in. Hold a sec, okay?" Heart pounding, she turned back to find Cole watching her with a funny look on his face. She handed him the beer and mouthed the words, "See you in an hour," before drawing her door closed.

Inside she put the phone back up to her ear. "Sorry about that. I'm back."

"I wanted to wish you luck tonight."

She doubted luck would have much to do with it, but still, she ought to acknowledge the courtesy. "Thanks, Randall, that's very thoughtful of you."

"You said you were just getting in. Where were you?"

Even if she hadn't stolen away to be with Cole, she liked to think that Randall's keeping tabs on her would have grated. Be it in business or in his personal life, her soon-to-be former fiancé was a control freak with a capital C.

"The cabinet voted this morning. There was nothing more I could do, so I thought I'd take a drive and do some sightseeing."

A long pause greeted that admission. "I trust Mr. Whittaker accompanied you on this...excursion?"

"Of course he did." She caught herself snapping and took a moment to modulate her tone before adding, "That's what a bodyguard does, isn't it?"

"Just checking to make certain he's earning the rather exorbitant fee he's charging me for his...services."

Until now, she'd all but forgotten that, like her, Cole was on Randall's payroll. Considering all that Cole's "services" had involved these past few days, she felt her face heating.

"Listen, Randall, I appreciate you calling, but I really need to get ready. We leave for the banquet in an hour."

"Very well, but know I'll be sitting here thinking of you."

Thinking of the billions the Belizean deal would bring in was more like it. "I'll call you as soon as I can break away, okay?"

"I'll be waiting. The staff of Sardi's has been informed that tomorrow night is a very special occasion. The sommelier has instructed his staff to put their best bottle of Dom Perignon on ice."

Alex hesitated. Little did he know it, but tomorrow night's dinner would be their version of the Last Supper.

Swallowing hard, she said, "When I get back tomorrow night, we really need to talk."

"Aren't we talking now?"

His arch tone surprised her, but she told herself he was probably just tense about the contract award. With billions of dollars at stake, that was certainly understandable. She didn't see how he could know about her and Cole. Even if Phillip Collins had seen them in the market earlier and reported back, an unlikely scenario, she'd already decided to break off her engagement. Really, what did any of it matter now?

His huff reminded her she hadn't answered him. "I really have to go. I'll see you tomorrow night."

She clicked off before he could keep her any longer and gave a guilty glance to the closed door. Opening the door would increase the air circulation considerably. Unfortunately it would also draw attention to the fact that she'd closed it in the first place so Cole couldn't overhear her conversation. At least the air conditioner was running. Someone must have fixed it while they were out.

Pulling her heavy hair up off her nape, she leaned in to the AC's blower, closed her eyes and took a moment to just breathe.

COLE SAT on the sofa, clenching the TV remote and staring at the cheesy Belizean soap opera on the tube without really watching. Once inside the suite, he hadn't wasted any time taking care of business, starting with a call to the local police non-emergency number to report the "accident" on Hummingbird Highway. He'd also placed calls into the main body shops in the area, promising the mechanics a hefty reward—okay, bribe—for any pertinent information. If, or rather when, someone brought in a white Bronco for repairs, he'd be getting a call.

Until the near collision on the road, he'd been more than halfway convinced that the note threatening Alex's life was a hoax. And then coincidentally or not so coincidentally he'd run into Tony at the resort. What were the odds? Still, there was no way the ex-con could have driven the Bronco and beaten him and Alex back to the hotel. Even if roadside assistance had been doing double time, it just wasn't possible. The only lead left to explore was also the most likely one—Phillip Collins. Before the end of the evening, he meant to find out where and how the Sun Coast executive had spent his afternoon.

For now though, he had little left to occupy his mind except for Alex. For the first time since she'd crossed the threshold on the night of their arrival, the connecting door was closed. She'd shut it as soon as they'd stepped inside, and he didn't have to wonder why, just as he didn't have to think twice about who the caller was. It was Traxton. When she'd clicked on that call out in the hallway, the shift in her had been instantaneous, her body visibly stiffening and at the same time seeming to shrink, her voice taking on the chilled, detached tone he hadn't heard since she'd boarded the jet in New York. He'd thought their lovemaking earlier might have changed things but apparently he'd only been kidding himself. It seemed she meant to uphold their bargain to the letter. After tomorrow, she'd say goodbye to Cole—and marry Randall Traxton.

Next door, he heard the shower going. With the clock ticking, he really ought to drag his sorry ass up from the sofa and do the same.

He raked hard fingers through his hair. Love made you weak. Love rubbed you raw. Love made you lower your guard. When lives were on the line, love was a damned dangerous state to be in. These last three days he'd felt as though he was being sucked beneath the surface of Alex's precious sinkhole. The harder he fought to keep his head above water, the faster gravity seemed to suck him under. In his case, gravity pretty much came down to the stark soulfulness of Alex Kendall's honey-brown eyes, her force-of-nature smile. He'd gladly undergo his HRT hazing a hundred times over, his arms pinned, his face masked, water pouring into his nose and mouth, than sign up for this kind of psychological torture.

The water board had nothing on the hell of having the woman you loved back in your arms and life again while knowing that in another twenty-four hours you'd be letting her go for good with nothing more than a goodbye.

EXACTLY forty-five minutes later Alex opened her door and crossed the threshold into the living room. Showered and dressed, Cole dropped the remote and shot up from the sofa, his gaze drinking her in. He'd expected her to look great, she always did, but seeing her framed in the doorway, he felt his heart tripping and his lungs locking.

Breathe, Whittaker, just breathe.

Dressed to kill in a chic, floor-length, red silk halter dress, wrist-high satin gloves, and strappy heels with some sort of glittery accent on the tops, she was beyond beautiful. Her eye makeup was understated to the point of transparency; her luscious mouth sported the shade of classic red lipstick associated with Hollywood starlets of the Silver-Screen era. Her hair was loose around her shoulders, an artful tumble of silky-soft waves that beckoned him to sift his fingers through them.

Feeling awkward and tongue-tied, he dropped his gaze to his hands. "You look…nice."

She lifted a pencil-darkened brow and crossed the carpet

toward him. "Just nice?" Reaching him, she grabbed him by his collar points and pulled him in for a kiss that likely left half of her lipstick on his face, not that he minded.

He drew back, her fragrance filling his senses. "You look beautiful. You are beautiful. I don't want to mess you up."

That made her smile. "Ever think that maybe I like it when you mess me up? Maybe I like it a lot."

A small red-satin purse dangled from her wrist. She unsnapped it and brought out a foil-wrapped condom. She tried handing it to him, but he shook his head. "We need to leave in the next fifteen minutes. If we do this, I can't guarantee you won't be late. Not making you late was your one big rule, remember?"

She shrugged, which did interesting things to the creamy cleavage tumbling out of her top. "Maybe I'm tired of rules, even mine—especially mine. Besides, why not look at the glass as being half-full rather than half-empty? We have fifteen whole minutes. Why not make the most of them?"

And then she did the unexpected. She tossed her purse on the coffee table, turned her back on him—and pulled her tight-fitting dress waist-high. Cole swallowed hard, blinked, but his mind wasn't playing tricks with him and neither, it seemed, were his eyes. Once again she wasn't wearing panties, not even a thong.

Bent forward and bracing the back of a chair, she tossed her hair out of her eyes and sent him a sexy smile from over one alabaster shoulder. "Clock's ticking, cowboy, and in case you're wondering, I'm already wet."

Cole hadn't thought he was still shockable, but he'd been wrong. "Let me get this straight. You want me to take you from behind without any foreplay whatsoever."

She nodded, her perfect pale ass tilted north and all but shoved up in his face, the angle affording him a teasing glimpse of the shadowed hollow between. If she could be believed, those still-hidden sweet lips were already wet and ready for him. "You can have all the foreplay your heart desires after the banquet. For now, this is the best I can offer. Just sex, take it or leave it."

Just sex—the words were like the key to his personal Pandora's Box. Suddenly the key turned, the lid lifted and he got it. From her point of view, he was one step up from a gigolo. She could use him for sex and then walk away—and right back to Traxton—without so much as a thought. Hadn't she said as much when she'd come into his room that first night? And yet even then he'd fooled himself into thinking they were making love. Earlier at the waterfall he could have sworn the final barrier between them had broken down, bringing about both a new understanding and a return to the old soul-deep connection. But the joke was on him. As far as Alex was concerned, they'd been having sex, just sex all along. Well, if she wanted soulless, no strings attached fucking, he would more than accommodate her.

He wedged a leg between hers. "In that case, spread your legs. Wider. I mean really wide." She started, no doubt surprised by his sharpness, and he took advantage of her reaction to slide a squeezing hand between the firm full lobes.

He bent and locked his mouth over the hot shell of her ear. "According to that wall clock, we're down to twelve minutes. Twelve minutes is just enough time for me to make you come once, maybe twice. But don't worry, I won't mess you up."

Straddling her from behind, he laid a heavy hand of the back of her slender neck, swept her hair to the side, and bit into her nape. She moaned and shoved back against his hips. "Cole, please—"

"Patience." Her soft sigh confirmed the plea was for him to continue, not stop. "You like it like this, don't you, baby?"

For the time they had left, the generic endearment was all she'd get from him. No more calling her Lex. That woman didn't exist anymore, at least not outside the box of his memories.

"Y-yes."

He slid his hand forward, his fingers slipping in her slickness. Sliding two fingers inside her, he tore open the condom packet with his teeth. He drew back long enough to roll down his zipper and cover himself.

She was bucking back against him, totally into it, really getting off. "Chalk it up to all those profiling courses I took at the FBI Academy, but I'd bet my former badge you're a switch, and whether you want me as the bottom or top, either way I'm more than happy to go along for the ride." He cinched his hands on her hips and pulled her back hard into him, impaling her in one iron thrust. Even in the midst of his passion, he couldn't seem to turn off his brain. "How does it feel to be treated like a flesh-and-blood woman and not some trophy-wife-in-the-works, arm candy for Traxton to flaunt in front of his business rivals?"

She didn't answer him. Her fingers clawed at the chair back. Through the silk of her dress, her skin felt moist and very hot. No longer caring whether he messed her up or not, he pulled out and thrust into her again. A few more strokes had her coming, the spasms rocking her so hard and deep that she swayed, almost fell off her heels.

Still inside her, he wrapped a steadying arm around her waist. "When we get back, are you going to recommend to Boyfriend that he give me a bonus? You know, for going above and beyond the call, for service with a smile."

This time she turned her head to look back at him. "Why are you being this way?" She reached around to pull down her dress, but he grabbed hold of her, his fingers banding her fragile wrist, and forced her hand back to the chair.

They really were out of time, and if he couldn't finish and find his own release, he'd settle for fucking with her mind. "I'm just upholding my end of our bargain. Four days of blow-out sex, just sex. That was what you wanted from me, isn't it? We only have a few hours left unless you're planning on us doing it on Boyfriend's plane." Still hard, he withdrew, yanked down her gown, and turned her around to face him.

Standing in the circle of his arms, amazingly she didn't push him away. Instead she lifted confused, wounded eyes to his face. Bravado gone, she looked close to crying. "Cole, please—"

He swept the pad of his thumb just below her lower lip, wiping away a smudge of lipstick. "No first names, remember? We should have stuck to that rule at least. It would have kept things in better perspective." He handed her the purse and looked beyond her to the wall at her back. "For now, though, we have the not-making-you-late rule to uphold. According to that clock behind you, you have exactly one and a half minutes to fix your face."

12

The National Assembly

You're in danger. Meet me in the coatroom—NOW!

ALEX REFOLDED Cole's note and slipped it beneath the scalloped side of her silver dish of lemon sorbet, a palate cleanser between the main course and dessert. Once the chocolate trifle made its way from the kitchen, the evening program would commence—and the contract award for the smart bacteria would be announced.

Cole must be really upset because the words on the oily scrap of hotel stationery might have been penned by a middle-school student, the loping letters out of synch with the cool, collected, detail-oriented man she'd spent the past three days rediscovering.

She cast her gaze to the back of the room where Cole stood watching her. She tried catching his eyes but, once she did, his inscrutable expression conveyed nothing. Then again, he was the consummate professional, trained to keep his emotions under wraps. Her thoughts cycled back to that afternoon's terrifying episode on the highway and her stomach flipped. Could he have discovered the driver's identity already and need to warn her of some new threat?

I'd be very interested to know how and where our buddy Phil spent his afternoon.

She felt eyes raking her and looked across the room. From one table over, Phillip Collins's gaze met hers. He raised his wineglass in mock salute, his smarmy smile in place, and she shivered despite the sticky air.

"Beastly climate." The droning British-accented voice drew her attention back to her seatmate, the wife of a retired British diplomat. "One might think I would have become accustomed to it by now, but after twenty-five years in Belize, I still yearn for the green fields and gentle rains of Kent."

Well, good luck with that. Alex set her napkin beside her plate and pushed back from the table. "You'll have to excuse me, please."

The Brit paused in dabbing at her forehead with the corner of her napkin. "Wherever are you off to?" Rivulets of rouge ran down her wobbly cheeks, staining the white satin piping of her gown pink.

"The powder room," Alex lied, needing to be on her way.

The woman's heavily penciled brows shot to her hairline. "But, my dear, the contract announcement is to be made in just a few moments. Can't you possibly wait?"

Sucking in her sides, Alex managed to squeeze out of the wedged-in seating. "I'm afraid not. Those Kegel exercises can only carry a girl so far."

The woman's jaw dropped. Alex turned and walked away but not before a hissed exclamation of "Bloody Americans" found its way to her ears.

Hugging the wall, she made her way down the aisle, scanning the diners seated at the white-cloth-draped banquet tables and the waiters congregating near the entrance to the kitchen. Cole was close by, she felt sure of it. Regardless of whether he was still angry with her, the desertion scene at the airport five years ago would never be replayed, not now, not ever. Accepting that as fact felt tremendously healing.

With a lighter step, she made her way out of the banquet room toward the foyer, Reaching the main stairway, she glanced back to make sure no one had followed. Fortunately, there was no one around to notice her.

The cloakroom was just inside the foyer, the door closed. There hadn't been an attendant earlier nor was there one now. But then Belmopan was surrounded by tropical rainforest. It wasn't as though guests arrived with Burberry trench coats and mink stoles to check.

Trusting that Cole must be mere steps behind her, she opened the door and stepped inside. The close space within was stifling and no doubt ripe with mold. Then again, she hadn't come for the scenery.

She drew the door closed behind her. "Cole?"

"GOING SOMEWHERE, Collins?"

Phil's rising at the very moment Alex exited the room might be one hell of a coincidence, but Cole wasn't taking any chances. Standing in the vestibule outside the banquet room, he planted his hands on the Sun Coast executive's lapels.

Collins was sweating big time, but for a guy whose back was against the wall—literally—he held it together pretty well. "I thought I'd take a leak, not that it's any of your business."

Cole cocked his head to the side. "You decide to take a piss right before the big announcement?"

Collins awiped his hand across his upper lip. "I've had a lot to drink."

Catching a whiff of the guy's breath, Cole confirmed that

this part of his story was true. "Where were you this afternoon?"

"That's none of your business, either."

Cole shrugged. "I can always beat it out of you after the banquet. For now, let's get you back to your seat before the big event."

"But I really have to go!"

The desperation in Collins's voice almost had Cole believing him. "Look at it this way, buddy. If you pee your pants, everyone will chalk it up to the excitement."

EYES ADJUSTING, Alex looked around. A few light evening wraps shimmered in the near darkness, but otherwise the metal racks were mostly bare, the hangers empty. A trickle of unease slipped down her spine. She'd give him another minute, two tops, before heading back. In the meantime, she could really use some light.

A pull cord dangled from the light fixture above her head. Unfortunately the ceiling was high, a good twelve feet. Rising up on her toes, she reached up with both arms, the tail of oily twine tickling her fingertips. Close, so close.

Something bruising grabbed hold of her, coiling about her waist and hauling her backwards. At the same time, a ham-sized hand clamped over her nose and mouth, a stinging stench of that brought back vague memories of high-school chemistry lab burning her nostrils and throat. Feeling as if her head had disconnected from her body, her arms and legs melting away like warm wax, still she fought back. She bit down, teeth sinking into a meaty, latex-covered palm. She gagged—and then the world went black.

TONY LOOKED DOWN at the woman slack in his arms and wondered if maybe he hadn't bitten off more than he could chew. But not more than *she* could chew, apparently. Who could have guessed the little bitch would go Hannibal Lecter on him before passing out? He turned over his seriously throbbing palm and wondered if he might need a rabies shot or at least some stitches. For the moment, though, he had bigger worries—how to get her out the door and into the truck before Whittaker figured out she hadn't just skipped out to powder her nose and came looking.

Leaning her upright against him, he dug his free hand into his pocket and pulled out the dinner napkin he'd swiped earlier. Using his teeth, he wrapped the cloth tourniquet-style around his wounded hand and finished it off with a neat knot. Problem solved for now, he swung her up into his arms. Fortunately she wasn't heavy, but she was tall with long legs and arms that flopped around now that she was essentially dead weight.

Slowly, quietly, he moved toward the door. Cracking it open, he confirmed the coast was clear. He headed out. The kid stationed at the front door in charge of parking cast him a brief, questioning look but fortunately he understood enough English to get the words *drunk* and *needs some air.*

He lumbered out into the twilight just as the catering truck drove into the pull-up, a chef-suited Irma behind the wheel. He cracked a smile. With the bucks from this job, they could disappear for good if they felt like it. But what the do-gooders, the so-called "societal successes," never seemed to get was that being bad wasn't all about the score.

For guys like Tony, crime was the toughest job he'd ever love.

DIVIDING HIS gaze between Phil shifting in his seat and Alex's empty chair, Cole couldn't take it any longer. He cut through the aisles between tables and headed for the door he'd seen

Alex leave by. When he'd first seen her get up, his gut had told him to go after her. He hadn't. He'd let his personal feelings—okay, his wounded pride—get in the way of doing his job. That was the very reason that as a bodyguard he'd never once let himself get involved with his principal—until now. Involved? Who was he kidding? He was in love with the woman. That she apparently only saw him as a sex toy suddenly didn't seem to matter. He loved her, unconditionally and completely, and unlike five years ago, he wasn't going to just walk away.

This time Cole was going after his girl.

A THOROUGH search of the main floor, including the women's restroom, turned up nothing. Alex was nowhere to be found. Heart pumping, Cole barreled out onto the veranda. He spotted the Mayan kid who'd valet-parked their car when they'd arrived and walked on over. "The woman I came in with earlier, the tall blond American, any chance you've seen her?"

"*Sí.* The beautiful señorita in the red dress, she have too much drink. The big American, he had to carry her out."

Alex's voice filtered back to him. *I never drink at these things.*

Tonight was no exception. Watching her from across the room, he'd only seen her take a few sips from the various wines served. If Alex was passed out, it wasn't from drinking. She'd been knocked out or drugged.

Beneath his tuxedo he felt sweat slide down his back and knew this time it had nothing to do with the temperature. It was basic instinct, raw animal fear. Fear for the woman he'd once meant to make his mate, the woman he loved still. Alex.

He swung back to the boy and demanded, "How long ago? Did you see where they headed? Did he put her in a car? What kind of car?"

The kid stared up at him, clearly clueless. Heart pounding like a steel drum, Cole reined in the impulse to grab him by the shoulders and shake the information loose. He'd been acting on emotion for days now, ever since Alex had first walked into Traxton's office in New York. Standing on the terraced entrance with sweat streaming into his eyes and his heart doing double time to break through his chest, he didn't have to think twice about where following his heart had led him.

Go to Belize and you're dead.

He'd failed Alex again, only this time instead of hurting her heart, his loving her just might have cost her her life.

Breathe, Whittaker, just breathe.

Cole raked a hand through his damp hair and repeated the questions in Spanish. Shrugs and confused looks met his queries, no doubt a reflection of his poor foreign-language skills. The best intelligence a fistful of American twenties could buy was that the "big American" had taken Alex around the back of the building, ostensibly so she could be sick. Cole would have shot the whole wad in his wallet, but it clearly wasn't going to help. Beyond "big" and "American," the kid didn't seem to remember much of anything.

An elderly couple stepped out on the balcony, the man hailing the valet. Cole recalled that the woman had been seated beside Alex.

Judging from the frown on her fleshy face, she was put out about something and insisting on leaving early. "No dessert at a formal dinner. I've never heard of such nonsense."

"Harriet," the husband countered with a patient smile,

handing the valet his ticket stub, "the catering vehicle going missing was an unforeseen circumstance."

Cole snapped to attention. "Excuse me, but did you just say the catering truck is missing?"

Pushing between them, the wife answered for him. "Not missing but pinched. Someone went out onto the back balcony for a smoke and saw the sous chef and one of the servers driving away in it."

Cole shot down the steps. From studying the blueprint, he knew the building like the back of his hand. He raced around the side of the structure to the back entrance used for food deliveries. The white catering truck he'd seen earlier was indeed gone, and his gut told him that the desserts inside weren't all that had been stolen.

ALEX CAME AWAKE in a small, low-ceilinged room. The taste inside her mouth reminded her of the nontoxic paste she'd sampled back in the first grade, the stuff that looked like cauliflower and tasted like glue. Stacked crates and brown shipping boxes lined the moisture-stained cinderblock walls. She was sitting in, or tied to, a ladder-backed and very uncomfortable chair, her arms pulled behind her, her wrists bound with duct tape. Duct tape—that was going to feel really good coming off. Then it hit her. It might not be coming off because she might not be getting out of here.

Before coming to Belize, she hadn't given the threatening note she'd received more than a passing thought. She'd been so sure it was a hoax, but she'd been wrong, so very wrong. Then again she'd been wrong about a lot of things. She'd needed a bodyguard after all. She needed Cole.

What a fool she'd been to leave the banquet. She should have known Cole would never lead her to a remote location, a coat closet no less. What had she been thinking? She hadn't been thinking, not tonight and not for the past few days, which was the crux of the problem, of course. She might be thirty-five, but she'd been acting as if she wasn't a day over sixteen—so much for counting on age and wisdom to come as a package deal.

A cough caught her attention, drawing her gaze over to the corner occupied by her kidnapper. Seated on a stool wobbling beneath his weight, he was shoveling chocolate trifle through the mouth hole in his ski mask. A ski mask— talk about cliché.

"These chocolate puddings are delish." The accent marked him as a New Yorker, probably from one of the boroughs beyond Manhattan—the Bronx or maybe Queens. He glanced over at her. "Want some?" He reached into the catering box at his feet and pulled out another plastic container.

Alex shook her head, for once not even tempted. Who would have thought she'd be kicking her chocolate cravings cold turkey. "Thanks, but I've learned to 'just say no.'"

He laughed at that. "For a white-bread broad, you're okay."

"Thanks." If things went south, it would make an interesting epitaph for her tombstone.

Tossing the empty dish aside, he got up and walked over to her. Alex tensed. Leaving her alone, he reached up toward the ceiling fan wheezing overhead. He jerked the chain several times, but like everything she'd so far seen in Belmopan, the appliance was apparently stuck on slow.

Sweating bullets that combined with his cheesy cologne to create an odor that would make sewers smell sweet, he backed away. "Fucking piece of crap's broke."

The potty mouth didn't make her blink, but bad grammar was the equivalent of nails raking down a chalkboard. Even in her current predicament, she couldn't resist correcting him. "The fan isn't broke, it's *broken*."

He shrugged. "Whatever. It must be like 120 degrees in here."

He pulled off his mask. His flabby face dribbled sweat, the short spikes of dark hair plastered to his bullet-shaped head. It was the man from the resort's cabana bar, the man Cole had been talking with when she'd come back from the bathroom.

His deep-set eyes connected with hers, horror spreading over his features as he realized the mistake he'd just made. He slapped a hand over his broad forehead. "Holy shit, Irma's going to kill me when she gets back from ditching the truck."

Alex fought against the fear threatening to overtake her. She couldn't say how long she'd been passed out, but the room's single small window showed it to be dark outside. By now Cole would be searching for her. Belmopan wasn't very big. He should be getting close. From his bio posted to the Guidepost website, she knew he'd worked some pretty high-profile domestic and international terrorism cases. He'd been a principal player in cracking more than a few. Her kidnapping should be a cakewalk for him, or at least that's what she wanted to believe.

Then again, he wasn't superhuman. Even before she'd found out about his FBI background, he'd always seemed a little larger than life to her. Maybe that had been the problem, her problem, all along. She'd cataloged men as either frogs or princes with nothing, no shades of gray in between. Cole wasn't a frog, a prince or some action-adventure super hero. He was an amazing man but still as mortal, as fallible as she was.

A shadow covered her. A droplet of warm water struck the bridge of her nose. She jerked her gaze back up to the big man's sweating face.

His frightened eyes bore down on her, his expression almost apologetic. "I'm real sorry."

Holy shit indeed.

COLE HADN'T lost any time in calling in Alex's kidnapping to the local police. The police tail on the catering truck had led them back to market square. Once they had Tony's wife in custody—the woman who'd run into him in the hotel lobby earlier—she'd sung like the proverbial canary. Apparently, even when the culprits were married, there was still no honor among thieves. The warehouse where Alex was being held was on the other side of the market square, not far from where they'd bought her Birkenstocks the other day. The irony was the whole time he'd been looking for her she'd been just a few blocks from their hotel.

Pistol drawn, Cole kicked out at the weathered wood. The door gave way on the third kneecap-jarring assault.

"Freeze!" The first thing he saw was Tony Sumatra's broad backside looming over Alex. "Drop your weapon and hands in the air."

Tony's hands shot into the air. "Shit, I guess this means I'm going back inside, huh?"

"I guess so. Now turn around and face the wall. You know the drill."

Cole swung his gaze to Alex. Seated in a chair, her wrists tied with duct tape, she looked bedraggled but unhurt—and seriously glad to see him.

He walked over to pat Tony down, starting by slamming him face-first into the wall. "Tony, Tony, did you think you could take in your rental Bronco to a repair shop, and I wouldn't find out? Even if it was registered in your wife's maiden name, I was bound to trace it back to you. As for hijacking that catering van, I don't mind telling you, there are some pretty high-powered people at that banquet pissed off about not getting dessert."

Slapping handcuffs on Tony, he kept a close eye on Alex. Tears, shakes and getting physically sick were all normal reactions in the aftermath of a trauma. Lucky for him, she showed no emotion but relief. He'd never been good with female tears, but Alex crying was his personal kryptonite. Keeping the pistol trained on Tony, Cole stepped behind her and got busy with the Swiss Army knife he'd brought.

His gaze snagged the spray bottle of Windex left out on the windowsill. He grabbed it and went down on one knee beside her. "I'm an ace at getting this stuff off, so try to relax." He turned the cleaner cap to the spray setting and started dousing the tape.

"Why is it I feel like I'm in *My Big Fat Greek Wedding?*" Turning her head to the side, she tried for a smile.

Duct tape didn't exactly feel good going on, but coming off, it hurt like hell. The preferred removal method was fast, really fast. Fortunately the cleaning solvent would dissolve the adhesive somewhat. He cut the tape free of the chair and then peeled away one edge from Alex's wrist.

"On the count of three, okay?"

She swallowed. "Okay."

He'd taken the industrial-strength tape off any number of rescued hostages, but Alex wasn't just anyone. She was the woman he loved, and if he waited any longer, he just might lose his nerve.

"One…" Cole yanked back the tape.

The adhesive tore free. Alex, however, didn't let out a sound. Cole looked down at the raw patch on her right wrist and felt rage well up inside him. Tony had better get busy saying his prayers.

Alex sent him a stoic smile. "Whatever happened to three?"

He touched her cheek. "I lied. By the way, you won."

"Excuse me?"

"The contract to develop the bacteria—you won it."

"You mean Traxton Biotech won it."

"No, I mean *you* won it. The Prime Minister and Cabinet were blown away by your presentation the other day." Taking advantage of her distraction, he pulled back on the second piece of tape.

This time she let loose with an "Ouch."

"You okay?" He got up and held out his hand.

"Peachy." She wrapped her hand around his, and he pulled her upright.

When he looped his free arm around her waist, she didn't move away. Earlier, when he'd first realized she'd gone missing on his watch, the guilt had come in as a close second to his primary emotion—fear. Now that the physical danger was past, the prospect of losing her again from his life scared the hell out of him, but it was too late to take back his feelings. When it came down to it, love wasn't really a choice, it just... was.

Close by, sirens blared. Cole answered the silent question in her eyes. "Your carriage awaits, Cinderella, or in this case your police escort back to the banquet." He dug into the jacket pocket of his tuxedo, rumpled like the rest of him, and handed her the folded paper on which she'd printed out her acceptance speech.

She stepped back to look at him and shook her head. But her mouth was smiling, her eyes, too. "You're amazing, do you know that? I'm not sure what to say."

Cole was at a loss for words. He'd accepted FBI Medal of Honor and lesser commendations from various law-enforcement and government agencies as a matter of course and without much real thought. Who would have thought that one compliment, one smile from Alex Kendall would have him tongue-tied and, yes, blushing?

"For right now say goodnight and good luck." He gave her a light kiss and a push toward the door.

Evening gown dragging, she started toward it, and then turned back. "Aren't you coming to, you know, guard me?"

Her trust in him warmed his heart even if it was misplaced. Since they'd landed in Belize, he'd made more rookie mistakes than he had when he was an actual rookie. Once he got back to Denver, he wasn't looking forward to writing up his trip report. Mike, Sal, Lester and Jake might not say anything to his face, but for certain they'd be scratching their heads and wondering what the hell had happened to him. Cole couldn't help but wonder himself.

Alex had happened to him, that's what. It was obvious he couldn't think clearly around her, couldn't do much thinking at all. His lady was so unfailingly beautiful, brave and honest, he didn't just love her, he admired the hell out of her. His lady—for the next twenty-four hours, at least.

He shook his head. "You'll be okay on your own from here on. I'll see you back at the hotel." He cut his gaze to Tony, cowering in the corner. "For now, Mr. Sumatra and I have some catching up to do."

Watching her leave, he swallowed hard. Whatever happened from this point on, she really would be okay on her own. Cole wasn't so sure he could say the same about himself.

13

ALEX'S ACCEPTANCE SPEECH couldn't have gone better if she'd rehearsed for hours. Forcing herself to forget her ruined dress and bedraggled hair, she stepped up to the head of the main banquet table and accepted the contract award plaque from the Prime Minister's own hand.

An improvised dessert reception followed, featuring treats from a local chocolate shop. Although she never really ate or drank at business functions, her rumbling stomach announced an exception was about to be made. As it turned out, she was kept too busy shaking hands, responding to follow-up questions, and accepting congratulations to break away.

Even Phillip Collins walked up to wish her well. "I've got to hand it to you, Alex, you're the better man."

"And you're a jerk, Phil, but well, thanks." She softened the statement with a wink.

He hesitated, reached out and touched her hand. "Hey, if you ever decide to make a change, the weather in San Francisco beats the hell out of New York's any day of the year. Seriously, Alex, Sun Coast would welcome you with open arms—and so would I." His bloodshot eyes resting on her face held a pathetic, puppy-dog sadness.

Whoever had hired Tony to kidnap her, in that moment she knew it was most definitely not Phil. He might be a jerk, he *was* a jerk, but he wasn't an evil man. Like almost everybody, herself included, he was just trying to find his way—and messing up plenty in the process. Having made more than her share of mistakes lately—certainly over the past five years—she could afford to be compassionate.

"Thanks, Phil, but I don't think it would work out."

The Prime Minister caught up with her just as she was about to sneak a chocolate-covered strawberry into her mouth. "Congratulations, Miss Kendall. We look forward to many fruitful years of partnership to come. I trust you are fully recovered from your earlier mishap?"

A brief closed-door session had preceded the ceremony. During it, all parties had agreed it would be best for the project to avoid any public mention of the kidnapping. The official story for anyone who cared to press was that she had fainted from the unaccustomed heat.

"Yes, thank you. Our CEO, Mr. Randall Traxton, will be calling you first thing in the morning to express his deep thanks."

She would call Randall as soon as she got into the car and headed back to the hotel. Even though it was to announce their victory, she dreaded picking up the phone.

Though it was late, Alex left the assembly building to the flash and pop of cameras. A Belizean reporter flashing a press pass rushed up the steps towards her, followed by two cameramen.

Shoving his mike in her face, he asked, "Miss Kendall, can you please to address the rumors of your recent kidnapping?"

"Excuse me?" She was stunned. Apparently gossip was the one thing in Belmopan that traveled fast. Forcing a smile, she asked, "Really, do I look like someone who's been abducted?"

The man's face fell, no doubt as he saw his shot at a front-page byline fading to black. "You disappeared from the banquet for more than two hours. There is a witness, a car valet, who swears he saw you carried out."

"I'm afraid I'm not yet used to your humidity. I'm a New Yorker, you know. Now if you'll excuse me."

Without waiting for his answer, she turned and headed down the steps to her car. She couldn't wait to get back to her hotel suite—and, hopefully, Cole.

"MR. WHITTAKER, my officers will take over from here."

The Chief of Police had entered the warehouse just as Alex slipped inside the patrol car. Dragging his gaze away from the window, Cole turned to him and said, "I need five minutes." A quick glance over at Tony showed the felon had turned white beneath his tan.

The Belizean hesitated, drawing a long breath. "Very well, you have five minutes, no more and no less. Use the time well and take care to remember that the suspect, though a criminal, is still an American citizen."

Cole nodded. "I can accomplish a lot in five minutes."

Cole waited until they were alone and then turned back to Tony. "We can do this the easy way or the hard way. Under the circumstances I'm a fan of the hard way, but either way, you're going to give it up. For starters, who hired you?"

"I don't know."

Shoving his pistol in his pocket, he grabbed Tony by the back of his bullet-shaped head and proceeded to pound him into the wall. Though Tony outweighed Cole, most of that weight was gut flab. Gut punches, face punches, uppercut jabs to the chest, Cole was relentless. He combined every trailer-park dirty trick he'd picked up as a kid with the self-defense moves he'd acquired as part of his agent and HRT training.

Whoever said "the bigger they are, the harder they fall"

must have been acquainted with Tony. One final punch sent the ex-con slamming into the slimy wall.

"Okay, okay, enough already." Eyes pleading, Tony wiped the snot and blood from his busted nose with the back of his trembling hand. "The guy goes by Beethoven. That's all I know—honest! He's some bigwig with a biotech company in New York."

Kneeling down, Cole got up close and personal, right in the thug's face. Cole's mind wheeled back to earlier that evening when Alex's phone had gone off. Beethoven's Fifth was the ringtone she'd programmed for Traxton. Still, it didn't quite add up. Why would Traxton sabotage his own project, a project slated to bring in billions of dollars?

"New York?" he asked. "You sure you don't mean San Francisco?"

Tony shook his sweating head. "No, it's New York. The exchange he has me dial into is 212."

Red-hot rage ripped through Cole. Turning back to Tony, he demanded, "How much is he paying you?"

Through the mask of bruises, Tony rolled his eyes. "This is a joke, right? I know how you Feds operate. You're wearing a wire, trying to get me to incriminate myself."

Cole snorted. In Tony's world there were no good guys and bad guys. Everybody was equally bad and just working opposite sides of the fence. Looking at the thug's bruised and bloody face, feeling his knuckles begin to swell and stiffen, Cole had to admit maybe Tony wasn't that far off base.

"I'm not wearing a wire, but even if I were, you've already incriminated yourself. The way I see it, you won't need my help finding your way back to the pen. You'll land back there in another few months all on your own. Still, even without solid proof, one call from me to your parole officer is all it would take— Or I could square things with the police here, claim this is all one big misunderstanding. The choice is yours."

A tear squeezed out of Tony's mostly swollen shut left eye. "What do you want me to do?"

Cole shrugged, though his heart pounded like a hammer. "Relax, Tony. All I need you to do is make one simple phone call."

Manhattan, 2:30 a. m.

"SHE'S DEAD!" The flute of Crystal Randall had just poured landed in his lap, the champagne sopping the front of his trousers and the Persian carpet at his feet. "You weren't supposed to harm her, you moron. You were supposed to keep her out of the way until the contract was awarded to Sun Coast by default."

On the other end of the line, Tony was breathing as if he'd just run a 10K. "It was an accident. I didn't mean to. It just... happened."

Sweat broke out over Randall's body. "Where are you now?"

"Belize."

"Well, stay there. I...I have to think."

"I'm going to need some money."

Wiring money to a murderer, even one yet to be charged, wasn't high on Randall's to-do list. "I'll...contact you later. Until then..."

"Lay low, yeah, yeah, I know the drill."

Hanging up, Randall drew a bracing breath and forced himself to look objectively at the situation.

Ratcheting down his heart rate, he told himself that what was done was done. No sense in crying over spilt milk, as his mother would say. Alex was dead, and as unfortunate as that was, it couldn't be helped. Her death wasn't the end of the world, not *his* world at any rate.

Everything had gone swimmingly until six months ago when Biotech's board of directors had discovered the money he'd embezzled. They didn't have enough solid evidence to call in the law and even if they did, any public outing would bring about a drastic drop in stocks. Instead, they'd been pressuring him to step down, suggesting he suffered from Founder's Syndrome, breakdown and similar rot. It was then that he'd hatched his scheme to make sure the Belizean smart bacteria contract went to Sun Coast—and himself with it as his former rival's new CEO.

Tony's future looked decidedly less rosy. Fortunately, Randall had taken great care to keep their dealings as strictly cash transactions, so nothing could be traced. Even the number he'd given Tony to call was in another name.

Perhaps it was a relic of his humble beginnings but Randall despised waste. Alex's death was a waste, pure and simple. Beyond that, he was going to miss her. He'd really been rather fond of his ice princess. That she'd apparently had a fling with her bodyguard shocked him mostly because it seemed so out of character. But the photo Tony had sent him didn't lie. Given time, he would have forgiven her infidelity. What she brought to the table—beauty, brains and charm—more than outweighed one moral lapse. She really would have made him the perfect wife. By the time she realized he'd never give her that baby she so wanted—a vasectomy five years ago had seen to that—it would have been too late. Now it really was.

Randall rose. Stepping over the champagne flute, he headed for the bar. Considering the news he'd just received, champagne wasn't going to cut it.

This was definitely a Scotch occasion.

TONY CLICKED OFF on the call and turned to Cole. "I did okay?"

Cole nodded and clicked off the recorder. The voice on the other end of that call was Traxton's, no doubt about it. "You did better than okay. Tony, my man, you did real good."

ON THE LIMO RIDE back to the hotel, Alex called Randall.

"Alex, is it really you!" He all but shouted into the receiver.

It didn't seem that she'd awakened him. Wondering if he might be drunk, though she'd never seen him imbibe to excess, she said, "Of course it's me."

For the span of several seconds, the only sound coming from the phone's receiver was his labored breathing. "It must be past midnight there."

"You might say the evening veered off schedule."

For whatever reason, she couldn't bring herself to tell him about the kidnapping. If she told him now, he'd only grill her relentlessly and she was too tired—and too eager to see Cole—to go there. The news would keep until tomorrow evening when she was back in New York.

"Listen, I have good news. We won the contract."

He hesitated. "That's…splendid." As reactions went, his was decidedly low-key.

"I'll fill you in on the details tomorrow evening." Once business was dispensed, she'd call off their engagement and return his ring. That she'd accepted it in the first place was a grim testimony to how lonely and desperate she must have been feeling. For now, she slipped it off her finger and tucked it inside the zippered compartment of her purse. "I'm exhausted. I'm going to bed now. We can talk more about it tomorrow night."

She had her thumb on the button to end the call when he called her back. "Alex…"

She swallowed an irritated sigh. "Yes, Randall."

"I'm glad the night turned out so...well."

ALEX FOUND Cole standing out on the balcony of their suite. The heat had broken for now at least, the evening air so cool she could almost use a wrap.

She dropped the award plaque and her purse off in her bedroom and then headed outside. "Hey, you."

"Hey." He turned to greet her. "How did it go?"

She joined him at the railing. "Surprisingly well, but then accepting awards is always the easy part." It was the saying goodbyes that were so damn hard.

Spotting his busted knuckles, she opened her mouth to press for an explanation, and then clamped it closed again. She was neither his girlfriend nor his wife. He didn't owe her an explanation. He didn't owe her anything at all.

Bracing her forearms on the top of the railing, she stared ahead into the night. The parking lot below wasn't the most pic-turesque of views, but beyond it palm trees swayed in the breeze and a perfect full moon hung in the canopy of star-studded sky.

He turned to face her. "You worked hard. You should be proud of yourself."

"Thanks, I guess I am. At the same time it doesn't seem to matter so much now. Maybe I'm still in shock."

"It's okay to admit what happened scared the shit out of you. It sure as hell scared me." Intense blue eyes fastened on her face.

She hesitated, wanting to kiss him, wondering if she still had the right. "I didn't think anything scared you."

He shook his head as though she didn't quite get it. "You'd be surprised."

He took her in his arms and she breathed a satisfied sigh. He kissed her forehead, her closed eyelids, and the bridge of her nose. He lifted each of her hands, turned them over, and kissed the abraded skin on her wrists. Finally he kissed her lips.

Alex forgot to breathe, forgot to worry, forgot to do anything other than feel. Whatever the return to New York might bring, nothing and no one had the power to ruin or steal this completely perfect moment.

She opened her eyes and looked up at him. "Make love to me, Cole."

He didn't answer in words, only slid a hand to the zipper at the side of her gown and drew it slowly down.

Sometime later he picked her up and carried her inside to his room. They made love slowly and sweetly as they used to do. Afterward, Alex settled onto her side with a satisfied sigh.

He unwrapped his arm from around her waist, her backside pressed against him. "I'll be right back. Don't go anywhere."

"I couldn't if I wanted to." Her mouth curved into a sleepy smile. "After the past three days, I'll be lucky if I can walk to board the plane tomorrow."

Her matter-of-fact mention of tomorrow's flight back to New York sent his mood slipping. He pressed a kiss to the curve of her shoulder. "Don't worry. I'll carry you anywhere you want."

He got up to use the bathroom. When he came back, she was asleep. Curled on her side, she had her hands tucked pillow-style beneath her head. Her kiss-swollen lips wore the hint of a smile. Soft snuffling, part purring and part snoring, joined the alarm clock's steady ticking.

Sweet dreams, baby.

A cooling wind wafted through the window, the perfect balm to the night's heavy heat. Looking down on Alex, her sleeping profile framed by pale tendrils stirring in the breeze Cole felt a rush of tenderness. He peeled back a corner of the sheet and slid into bed beside her. Rolling onto his side, he gathered her against him, not wanting to wake her but selfishly needing the reassurance that skin-to-skin contact conveyed. Even in sleep, she sighed and melted into him. His heart flipped, constricted.

Fate had brought the best damned thing that had ever happened to him back into his life and his bed. He couldn't believe Alex had come back after five years only for a fling. Before they returned to New York, he needed to tell her about Traxton. He should have told her tonight, but the danger was past. Earlier, he'd e-mailed Les from his BlackBerry, putting in a request for some final fact checking. By the time their plane touched down in New York tomorrow, he should have pieced together the complete story behind Traxton's bizarre turn-about. Beyond that, selfishly, he'd just really wanted one more night to hold her.

He stretched out beside her and buried his face in the silk of her hair. "I love you, Lex."

Exhausted though he was, with his thighs pillowed against her perfect little bottom, he felt himself hardening. He couldn't get enough of her, but there were only twenty-four hours in a day and even he needed to use one or two of them for sleeping. Yet as he watched the shadows crawl across the peeling plasterwork, thinking of how close he'd come to losing her and all the ways he still might, it was a long while before he closed his eyes to sleep.

14

Friday, Day Four

ON THE plane back to New York, Alex and Cole said very little. Having perky Kim never more than a few feet away made for a subdued atmosphere. Cole spent a lot of the time with his BlackBerry, thumbing through e-mails and sending replies. Apparently he had already moved on and was ramping up for his next mission. Alex wished she could do the same but for her the last four days weren't so easily swept aside. She'd been hoping the kidnapping scare would jar Cole to make some declaration, but apparently that wasn't going to happen. Once they got back to the city, he would head for Denver and the next chapter of his action-adventure life. She, presumably, would return to corporate America—and Randall. She hadn't told Cole about her decision to end her engagement that night. She wanted his love—period. The last thing she wanted was for him to feel guilty or obligated to her in any way.

They landed to find the limo parked on the airstrip, ready and waiting. They deplaned to air that was knife-sharp and bitingly cold. The winter landscape looked as bleak as Alex felt. She shivered and turned up the collar of her coat. They climbed into the car and headed toward the city, the car heater at full blast.

Her apartment on Fourth Avenue was the first stop. Their driver drew up to the curb and put his blinkers on. To her surprise, Cole got out of the car with her. He took both their bags from the limo trunk, and then waved the driver off.

Alex wasn't sure what came next. Standing on the sidewalk fumbling for her key, she turned to him. "Day four isn't officially over until midnight. Do you, uh…want to come up?"

He hesitated, never a good sign. "Take a walk with me. I have something to say to you, and, well, you know I always think better on my feet."

He held out his hand and she took it. For the first time since the alarm went off that morning, she felt hopeful. Maybe things might work out between them after all?

They left their luggage with her doorman and walked to Fourteenth Street, then crossed Union Square East to the park. Cutting through, Cole walked in silence until they came up to the Lincoln statue all the way in the back.

He turned to her. "There are things you need to know about Traxton."

That was definitely not what Alex had hoped to hear. "What kinds of things?"

"Randall wrote that threatening letter. When that didn't scare you off from going to Belize, he hired Tony Sumatra to do his dirty work for him."

She couldn't believe what she was hearing. "Randall plays hardball when it comes to business, no doubt about it, but he's not a monster, and only a monster would do what you're suggesting. Besides that, why would he sabotage his own project, a project worth billions?"

"His board of directors was getting ready to give him the boot. Apparently they found out he was embezzling. At their next general meeting, they were going to vote him off the island, so to speak. Before that could happen, he cut a deal with Sun Coast to bring them the Belizean contract—and come over as the new CEO."

Alex's head felt ready to explode, the intense pressure sending the statue of the former president on a dizzying merry-go-round ride. "And my life was a small price to pay?"

Cole hesitated. "That day in his office I couldn't figure out why he was so insistent I handle the mission personally when everything about it was routine. It made me uncomfortable, wary, but before I could probe deeper you walked in and, well...I didn't follow my gut and find out why. Now I understand. Before I ever walked through his office door, he'd memorized not just Guidepost's corporate capabilities statement but my personal résumé. High-speed evasive driving happens to be a particular area of expertise for me, and he wanted to make sure I would be with you in that car when Tony came after us. He knew the odds were stacked in favor of me getting you out of that risk scenario not only alive but unhurt. If it makes you feel any better, he never meant for you to be hurt."

She braced a hand on the bench back and shook her pounding head. "It doesn't, but thanks."

"I have Tony's taped phone conversation, which clearly incriminates Traxton. With my testimony, we can put Boy... Traxton behind bars."

Alex shook her head. "The Belizean government would re-award the contract. There would be no choice. Randall notwithstanding, Traxton Biotech is still the best firm for the job. Even if we somehow managed to hold on to the contract, the bad press would overshadow the potential for good being done. With so many environments projected to be in future jeopardy from petroleum poisoning, killing this project would be an even greater crime. No, this is something I'd just as soon take up behind closed doors with the board of directors."

His arm found its way around her shoulders, a familiar comforting weight. "Okay, we'll play it your way, but if you change your—"

"I won't but thanks."

He cleared his throat. "Until his people tell him otherwise, Randall thinks you're dead. To get his confession, I had Tony tell him that he'd accidentally killed you."

Feeling dizzy, Alex shook her head. "Not anymore he doesn't." No wonder Randall had sounded so shocked to hear from her last night. "Before I got back to the hotel last night, I called to tell him about the contract award."

Cole paled. "Until we have Traxton under control, I don't want you going back to your apartment."

"I have to go back. It's my home. My cats are there!"

She lifted her gaze to Cole's face, the ruggedly handsome face she never seemed to get enough of touching and kissing and looking at, when the ugly truth hit her like the exploding pellets from a paintball gun. "You've known this for what, a day, and yet you said nothing until now!" His keeping secrets, not trusting her, making decisions that involved her without her knowing—it was five years ago on instant replay.

She waited for him to deny it, but he didn't. "I didn't want to frighten you or spring this on you before I'd checked out all the facts with my associates back in Denver."

She thought things had changed, that *he* had changed, but now she saw she'd only been kidding herself. His life was top secret—and his heart off-limits—as ever.

She let go of the bench and shoved away. "Goodbye, Cole. You have yourself a safe flight back to Denver and a nice life. I'll be just fine."

"Alex, wait."

He took a step toward, her but she shoved hard hands against his chest. "No more."

"Alex, please—"

She turned away and started walking. Dodging skateboarders and promoters shoving flyers in her face, she made her way out to the street.

Amazingly he followed, catching up with her on the sidewalk outside the bookshop. "Alex, please let me explain."

She whirled around. "I'm over it, Cole, all of it. I'm done with loving someone who will always use secrets to keep me at arm's length. I'm not going to waste another nanosecond of my life wrapped up in you."

MINUTES AFTER leaving Cole standing on the street, Alex set her luggage down inside her apartment door and slipped off her coat. She supposed he'd come back to collect his luggage from her doorman eventually. She told herself she didn't care.

The girls trotted across the living room to greet her. Alex squatted down to pet them. "Hey babies, was the pet sitter good to Mommy's girls?"

It occurred to her that her cats might well be the only two creatures in her life she could wholly trust. She certainly couldn't put her trust in men, not her slimeball soon-to-be ex-fiancé and not Cole, either. Apparently her mother had been right all along. There were no handsome princes, just better-looking, less-warty frogs.

She grabbed a bottle of water from the kitchen and made her way to the couch. Tessa hopped up on the cushion beside her. China scaled the sofa back and then settled on her lap. If only her relationship needs might be so easily met. If only men could be more like…well, cats.

Her cell phone went off, belting out Beethoven's Fifth. The sudden sound sent China flying off the sofa and scrambling for cover. Randall. She considered letting him leave a voice message, then chided herself for being twice a coward. It was time to face the music—literally.

She grabbed the cell and clicked on the call. "Why didn't you call me when you first got in?" His petulant voice poured out from the cell's receiver. Apparently he didn't have a clue that she knew. That was interesting.

She swung her legs over the sofa side and sat up. "I put my feet up for a few minutes, and I guess I fell asleep." It was a half truth, which was fifty percent more honesty than the bastard deserved.

His huff funneled through the cell's receiver. "I hope you don't mind but I've invited a third party to our dinner tonight. Oliver Woo of Kyoto Enterprises is in town for a brief visit. He flies back to San Francisco tomorrow morning. Tonight is our last chance to meet."

"But don't you want me to catch you up on my trip?" she asked, her tone saccharine-sweet.

He hesitated. "We'll have other nights."

I wouldn't be so sure of that, asshole.

"Dinner is at eight. I'll have my driver pick you up in an hour. Wear the silver-and-black Valentino, won't you, the one with the knitted half-sleeves?"

Alex knew it well. The dress had never really felt like "her," but she'd let Randall coerce her into wearing it as he had coerced her into so many other things. Funny how she'd never really confronted his attempts to control her before. Looking back, she supposed she'd been an easy mark, flattered to be on the receiving end of so much male attention.

Things weren't going to work out with Cole, but his

coming back into her life had saved her from a major mistake. It had saved her from Randall. Being alone was a lot better than being trapped into marriage with a conscienceless man, a criminal. Even though she wasn't going to get her fairy-tale ending, she felt fundamentally thankful.

"No."

"Excuse me?"

"I said no." This time her voice came out strong, her refusal manifestly clear.

He hesitated. "I've been wooing Kyoto Enterprises for six months now. This dinner is important to me."

Searching her memory, she realized that Kyoto had been a subcontractor to Sun Coast on several projects in the past. She didn't for a minute think the two CEOs' meeting for dinner was a social visit. Now that she'd won the Belizean bacteria contract for Biotech, presumably Randall's defection to Sun Coast was off. The dinner meeting must mean Randall had come up with a plan B.

His voice broke through her thoughts. "I have it from a very reliable inside source that Mr. Woo is a connoisseur of Western female beauty."

Even after all the crap he'd pulled, the blatancy of his suggestion sent Alex's jaw dropping. As if threatening her life and hiring someone to kidnap her wasn't enough, he figured since she was still around he might as well pimp her out to his business associate. Talk about gall!

"I'm not a whore, Randall." She glanced down at her wrists, the skin rubbed raw from the duct tape, and suddenly she was really, really looking forward to their evening.

He must have sensed from her silence that he'd finally gone too far because he started back-pedaling. "Face it, Alex, whatever else you are, you're also a lovely woman, and beauty is an asset to be manipulated like any other. You've never behaved so obstinately before. What's the matter with you?"

Beyond being almost run off the road and kidnapped, and now being brokenhearted and jetlagged, not a damn thing.

She took a deep breath and prepared to lie through her teeth. "You're right, Randall. I am being selfish, aren't I? Of course I'll have dinner with you and Mr. Woo, only I'll have to meet you there." He started to argue, insisting he'd send over the limo, but she held firm. "I'll see you there." She clicked off on the call and sat back.

Breathe Alex, just breathe.

She'd always enjoyed Sardi's, but tonight she wouldn't be going for the food.

THOUGH it was early yet, Sardi's was filling up fast. Across the crowded room, Alex spotted Randall ensconced at his usual booth. Seated across from him was a distinguished Asian man with salt-and-pepper hair, presumably Mr. Woo. She had to hand it to her almost-ex. He certainly rolled with the punches.

The maître d' greeted her with a smile and ushered her across the room. At her approach, the two men stopped talking and rose.

"Alex." Randall ran his gaze over her, a frown fighting with the Botox freezing his forehead.

Alex didn't have to guess at the source of his displeasure. She hadn't bothered to change. She still wore the linen pants suit she'd put on that morning, the fabric creased from hours of sitting. Other than running a comb through her hair, which she'd left loose, she hadn't done a damned thing to herself.

"Aren't you going to introduce me?" She shifted her gaze to Mr. Woo.

"Yes, of course. Allow me to present Alexandra Kendall, my Director of Research and Development."

"Miss Kendall." Mr. Woo inclined his head in Alex's direction, his dark eyes settling on her face. "If our companies decide to do business together, I assume you will be the main liaison with my R&D Director in San Francisco."

Alex shook her head. "I'm afraid not."

Out of the corner of her eye, she saw Randall flinch. "I should explain that Miss Kendall is also my fiancée. Once we marry next month, she'll be resigning her position at Traxton."

Mr. Woo divided his gaze between Alex and Traxton. "In that case, congratulations are in order."

"Thank you, Mr. Woo, but actually you might want to hold off." She swung around to Randall. No way was she going to risk missing the look about to come crashing tsunami-style over his face. "I'm not waiting to resign. I'm resigning effective immediately." She opened her tote and pulled out the envelope with her resignation letter addressed to his stockholders and board of directors. In it, she intimated that if they didn't act accordingly and terminate him on the spot, she'd be taking her story to *The New York Times.*

Randall pulled his disbelieving gaze from the envelope to search her face. "Alex, I don't understand."

His mouth hung open, bringing back memories of her one and only time fishing. Sighting the spot of blood where the hook had sunk in, she'd released the trout back into the water. Tonight, however, she felt considerably less kind.

"Then let me clear things up for you. Not only are you a

liar and a saboteur, but you're also a kidnapper, and if the bodyguard you hired had a fraction less expertise behind the wheel, you'd also be a murderer."

Red-faced, Randall swung around to Woo. "Alex is quite the comedian, particularly when she's imbibed. I'm afraid she must have hit the martinis pretty hard on the plane back from Belize." Teeth gritted, he made a grab for her hand. "Alex, sit down! I'll have the maître d' call my driver to take you home." He made a show of waving down a waiter.

She raised her voice the few decibels needed to carry to the patrons at nearby tables. "Sending me that anonymous death threat was a nice bit of stage craft, but it was only the beginning. When you couldn't scare me off going to Belize, you knew you needed to take stronger measures. Still, hiring a thug to run me off the road and then kidnap me was pretty over the top, and all so you could hijack the smart-bacteria contract and take it over to a rival company." She turned back to Mr. Woo, who wore a look of astonishment. "I came here because you have the right to know exactly what sort of man you'll be climbing into bed with if you entertain any business dealings with Traxton."

Recovering, Randall adopted a worried look and shook his head. "I'm afraid Miss Kendall is not only a substance abuser but delusional as well." He reached toward her, but Alex slapped his hand away. "Darling, we've gone over this all before, and you really must be better about taking your medication."

Alex snorted. "Nice try, but I'm guessing Mr. Woo isn't buying your crap, either. I'll be consulting an attorney tomorrow. If I do decide to pursue legal action, you'll be hearing from her shortly. And just in case you get any ideas about shutting me up, a friend of mine has you on tape talking to Tony about what a shame it was he ended up accidentally killing me."

She turned to go, stopped, and then swung around. Pulling her engagement ring out of her purse, she tossed it onto the table. "I guess this is as good a time as any to tell you the wedding's off."

IF ALEX had any second thoughts that maybe she'd gone too far, Mr. Woo following her out to the sidewalk outside Sardi's confirmed she'd handled the situation just right. Once inside their shared cab, he'd complimented her on her courage, thanked her for saving his firm from any association with such an evil, dishonorable man, and finally, offered her a job. The research and development position would be comparable to the one she'd just left, only at a higher salary. And it would require her to relocate to California.

Though honored to be asked, Alex didn't have to think twice. She declined. Despite Mr. Woo urging her to take twenty-fours to think things through, she held firm. The time in Belize had her reexamining her priorities, namely what she wanted to do with the rest of her life. Corporate America was no longer for her. It had never been a good fit but rather a place to escape to. The constant hyper-drive pace had let her block out the past by keeping herself not only busy 24/7 but emotionally numb.

By the time she got back to her apartment, she felt pretty proud of herself. She changed into jeans and an old T-shirt—Cole would definitely approve—and headed into the kitchen for a microwaveable meal and a glass of wine. She'd just finished pouring the wine when the intercom buzzer sounded. She turned away from the fridge and picked up.

Carlos, the night doorman, answered. "There's a Mr. Whittaker to see you. You want me to send him up?"

Her heart lurched. "No." Judging from rumblings in the

background, Cole wasn't just going to go away. "Put him on the phone please."

"But, Miss Kendall, only building staff are allowed to use—"

"Put him on please."

Cole's voice funneled through the receiver. "Alex, I—"

"Funny, I don't recall inviting you over."

"I was worried. I had to know you were all right."

Alex raked a hand through her hair, steeling herself against melting. "I am, so you can go now."

"Please, Alex, don't make this into a repeat of five years ago. Hear me out this time, and then if you still want me to go, I promise I'll leave, no arguments."

The reference to five years ago cinched it. She buzzed him up. Chest heavy, she stood at the door, listening for the elevator doors to open. They did. Muffled footsteps forged a path to her apartment door. She held back, making him ring the doorbell. He did. On the count of three, she opened the door.

"Thank you." Hollow-eyed and weary, Cole stared down at her and suddenly every rebuttal she'd rehearsed from that morning emptied from her head.

"Don't thank me just yet. I agreed to hear you out— period." Holding the door, she stepped back to let him inside.

He wore the same clothes he'd had on that morning with the addition of a charcoal-colored trench coat. Who would have thought a simple trench could look so…amazing?

Mewling drew their gazes down to the floor. The girls trotted up. All about the newcomer, they swished around his ankles and sniffed his outstretched hand. Crooning silly sweet nothings, he squatted down. Co-opting her cats—talk about the last straw. He was still the old Cole, still a charmer, and all that masculine mojo apparently worked on females regardless of species. Even China Boo-Boo, habitually wary of strangers, accepted him scratching beneath her chin as if they were old friends, the little traitor.

He stood and ran his gaze over Alex. "Jeans, huh? I was beginning to wonder if you owned any."

She folded her arms across her chest and stood her ground, determined to keep her distance and her dignity. "I thought you didn't like small talk."

"You're right. I came because I wanted to say…" He spread his arms wide, the long, thick fingers she knew so well combing the air.

Cole at a loss for words. That was new. In their Denver days he'd always seemed so sure of himself. Coming here must be hard for him, but for once Alex wasn't going to take responsibility for smoothing out the rough edges.

He drew a deep breath and then blew it out. "Christ, Lex, I came here to tell you I love you. I loved you five years ago, though I may not have ever gotten around to saying it."

She tightened her arms over her chest, armoring herself against the hurt. "As a matter of fact, you didn't."

"Well, I should have. I'd planned on it. After the mission, I was going to blow two weeks salary on taking you out to dinner at the Broker, order the most obscenely priced champagne on the wine list, and then go down on one knee and ask you to marry me, the *real* me."

Alex felt her eyes fill. Situated in an old bank vault, the romantic restaurant was all dark cherrywood paneling and stenciled glass and big leather booths. Cole had taken her there on their first official date. The meal, starting with a huge bowl of jumbo steamed shrimp, had been nothing short of amazing, but Alex had been too excited to do more than pick at her food, sip her wine and stare across the table into

Cole's shining eyes. Back then it had never occurred to her to question how a humble country-and-western band leader could afford Denver's flagship fine dining restaurant, but then it hadn't occurred to her to question much of anything.

She swiped a hand across her eyes, the bittersweet memory bringing buried feelings bubbling to the surface. "Okay, great, thanks for letting me know. You can go now." She reached around him to open the door.

"Alex—"

"Go!"

"Not yet. Not like this. I'm not going to just disappear from your life again, not even if you want me to. If this really is goodbye, then at least let me say goodbye—my way." Before she could move away, he swept her up in his arms.

EVEN AFTER he set her down, Alex didn't try pulling away or digging in her heels. She didn't resist in any way. Willing, complicit and, yes, weak, she stood before him with the bed bumping the backs of her legs and let him undress her, first her T-shirt and then her jeans.

He pushed her back on the bed, taking himself with her, covering her body with his. Even with the tears sliding back into her scalp, she couldn't wait to take him inside her.

A condom packet materialized in his hand. He drew back for the few seconds it took to cover himself. And then he was inside her, deep, deep inside, moving in a way she couldn't resist matching. She came hard, the contractions splintering her like a tree rent by a bolt of thunder. Cole followed. This time he wasn't quiet at all.

"Lex!" He flexed his hips and drove into her.

Afterward he stayed inside her for a long while. "My flight doesn't leave until tomorrow evening, another red-eye."

She rolled over on her side and got up. "In that case, bon voyage." Where he was concerned, her body and heart would always be weak, but this time she was determined to hold on to her will.

He swung his legs over the bed and started pulling on his shirt. "For the record, I realized after you left me in the park that I was wrong to keep the information about Traxton from you, flat-out wrong. You had every right to know up front. I should have told you after your acceptance speech."

"Yes, you should have." She found her T-shirt on the carpet and hurried to put it on, feeling vulnerable, exposed. "But it doesn't matter now. I've dealt with him. He wouldn't dare come after me." She briefly relayed the episode at the restaurant.

Shaking, she stepped into her jeans and pulled them up. "I still think you should let me turn in that tape, but—"

"The decision is still mine and the answer is still no."

Facing her across the mattress, he locked his gaze on hers for an unnervingly long time. "My plane doesn't leave until seven o' clock tomorrow evening. Think over what I've said, sleep on it, and if you feel any differently, call me. Better yet, meet me in Union Square Park at four o'clock. I'll wait for you by the Lincoln statue."

She tossed him his pants. "You're wasting your time."

He shrugged and then turned away to gather up the rest of his clothes. "It's mine to waste. I'll be there until four-fifteen. If you're a no-show, I'll catch a cab to JFK and still make my flight. You'll never have to worry about crossing paths with me again."

Suddenly anger overtook her. She stamped a socked foot into the beige wall-to-wall. "Damn you, Cole, I deserve more, a hell of a lot more. I deserve someone who can be there for me, really be there, and not just when you're between missions.

I won't settle for the crumbs from some all-consuming job, some higher calling after it's burned you out and bled you dry. And most of all, I won't settle for being lied to. I won't pretend not to know. Five years ago I probably would have but not now. Not ever again."

His eyes shot open. Fully dressed, he came around the foot of the bed toward her. Stopping inches short of touching her, he demanded, "Who's asking you to settle for crumbs? Who's asking you to settle—period?"

"That's just it. You don't ask. You expect." She shook her head. "For you it's always been about the game, living in the moment, but I need more than moments. I need to know you're going to be here beside me not just tonight or tomorrow but every day. I need to know you're not in some foreign country on an undercover assignment being tortured, or worse yet killed. I can't settle for the here and now anymore. I need to know there's a future I can count on."

He swiped a hand through his hair. "I can't promise you a storybook-perfect life, Lex. I can't promise you I'll be perfect. I'm probably about as far from perfect as a guy can get. What I can promise is that I'll always love you, and I'll always be there for you, just not in the 24/7 way you're holding out for."

"That's not good enough."

He blew out a breath and answered with a sad shake of his head. "If I've learned anything over the years, it's that the present is all any of us can count on. Whether I'm a secret agent or a bodyguard or a retail clerk, in life there are no guarantees."

15

AFTER LEAVING Alex, Cole spent a restless night back at his hotel. The next day was even worse. He picked up his cell to call her not once but several times. Every time he closed the case and shoved the phone back in his pocket. It wasn't his place to persuade her, and God knew he was done with pretending to be anyone other than who he was. For things to work out between them, she'd have to take him for himself.

He packed up early and stowed his suitcase with the concierge. Though he had hours free to explore the city, there was only one place he wanted to be. He climbed the stairs from the Union Square subway stop a full hour early. Unlike the day before, the sun shone, though without the blistering intensity he'd accustomed himself to over the past few days. After the sweltering heat and humidity of Belize, the gentle rays and crisp autumn air were a welcome balm.

The park was packed, an open-air market in progress. The crowd congregating around the canopied stalls carried him back to market day in Belmopan and his heart tightened. Regardless of how the afternoon ended, he'd be forever grateful for the memory of Alex twirling about in her colorful clothes, bright-eyed and beaming, as happy as she was meant to be.

With time on his hands, he started walking. He came upon the Strand. A New York City institution, the Strand bookstore occupied the corner of University Place and 12th Street, close to a city block. Owing to the ubiquitous sidewalk sale, the 12th Street side was clogged with people browsing the carts of discounted books. Cole could see why. Forty-eight cents for a paperback and a buck for a hardback—you couldn't beat those prices anywhere, but in the heart of Manhattan, they counted as crazy. And try as he might, he couldn't shake the black feeling he'd be needing reading material for the plane.

He slipped into the throng, thumbing through the hardbacks. The title *Free Fall* caught his eye but it was the author's name, Alexandra Kendall, in big black block letters on the spine that had him snatching it off the rack before the woman beside him could get her mitts on it. Chest tight, he shoved the book beneath his arm and went inside to pay.

Standing in line by the register, he read the back cover. Shit! This wasn't fiction, it was real life, his and Alex's story of five years ago! The female protagonist was a wannabe songwriter, not a novelist, but otherwise she was Alex to a T. And the "handsome as sin" country-and-western singer who'd deserted her and broken her heart was him down to his Stetson and snakeskin boots.

By the time he hurried back over to Union Square, the benches were filling up fast, the ones by Lincoln all taken. He backtracked and cut down a set of side steps to the street level where the crowd was thinner. For the time being he sat down by the gated statue of Gandhi. Tucked away behind a vendor selling black-and-white prints of various city scenes and some seriously bad acrylic art, he opened Alex's book to the first chapter. The flashback was written in the first person, and it didn't take much imagination to hear her voice narrating the scene.

I stood at the airport gate, my limbs no longer shaking but slack, my dropped bags lying like dead soldiers at my feet, the cruel reality crashing down on me more than compensating for their missing weight. Cooper wasn't coming for me, he wasn't ever coming for me, and his absence couldn't be blamed on a car accident, a traffic tie-up or a brush with the law. He wasn't coming because he didn't love me. Whatever his feelings, they'd run their course in what for me had been an all too brief four weeks, for him, though, a time obviously sufficient, more than enough.

Cole stopped. Tears dampened his eyes, and his throat thickened. A fat droplet struck the page, causing the words to blur. He closed the book, unable to go on. For the first time, he realized how profoundly he'd hurt her.

Second chances were rare as four-leaf clovers or shooting stars. He hoped to God he hadn't blown his. He didn't want to think of himself thirty or forty years out, sitting in some assisted-living activities room wearing adult diapers and brooding over Alex Kendall, the one who got away.

He couldn't go back in time and undo the past, but the present and more importantly the future were still up for grabs. He still had a chance—provided Alex would give it to him.

ALEX STOOD at the glass picture window in her apartment's living room, China Boo-Boo and Tessa stretched out and sunning on the sill. If she angled her head just so, she could glimpse a sliver of the northwest quadrant of the park. She couldn't see Lincoln from this vantage point or Cole either, but like the statue, she knew he would be there, waiting.

I can't promise you a storybook perfect life, Lex. I can't promise you I'll be perfect.

Did she expect perfection from others, Cole especially?

She hadn't thought so but she was no longer so sure. Life provided few if any guarantees, but it did offer opportunities, sometimes even second chances, to those brave enough to reach out and take them. She swung away from the window and marched toward the door.

Breathe, Alex, just breathe.

She pulled her coat out of the closet, grabbed her key and headed out into the hallway. Like a watched pot reluctant to boil, the elevator seemed to take an eternity to arrive. Once it did, she stepped on, grateful for the solo ride. Stepping out into the lobby, she realized she'd left her cell phone back upstairs. Shit!

Meeting up with the daytime doorman, she asked, "What time is it?"

"Ten after four."

There wasn't time to go back for the phone but five minutes should be time enough to make it to the statue provided she hurried. Union Square was kitty corner from her building, but Alex wasn't taking any chances. In addition to the usual crowd clogging the subway stairs, there were the market-goers to deal with. Knocking shoulders and skirting slowpokes, she walked down Fourth Avenue and then cut across Union Square East. High heels grinding the sidewalk to gravel, she reached the square in what had to be record time. Skirting the stalls lining the Fourteenth Street side entrance, she raced up the terraced steps toward the statue of a mounted George Washington. Heart tripping over itself, she cut to the left, bypassing the circle and making for the main cut-through. Benches lined either side of the path, their occupants a potpourri of incognito celebrities in dark sunglasses, baseball caps and floppy-brimmed hats, NYU students, young moms with strollers, drugged-out panhandlers and homeless war vets.

Bypassing the fenced-in dog park and the jungle gym, she

made a beeline for the Lincoln statue. Her usual bench was taken up by a twenty-something couple inhaling each other's faces, a pair of snowflake poodles perched patiently at their feet. She looked around. No sign of Cole. Had she missed him? Had he deserted her again?

Given their history, the latter wasn't a far-fetched conclusion to come to, and yet something inside her wouldn't let her go there again, wouldn't let her give in to the hopelessness. She retraced her steps, scouring the picnic tables and patches of lawn where intrepid New Yorkers soaked up the year's last tepid rays.

Heart sinking, she walked slowly back toward the front of the square. A shouted "Timber!" drew her gaze downward to the street level. She hesitated and then started down the side steps to the stalls set up on the sidewalk along Union Square West. Two men carried one of the tented tables away. Behind it, a shaft of sunlight struck a head of silvery hair.

Cole sat on the heretofore hidden bench, a closed book in his lap, the gated statue of Gandhi at his back. Seeing him there was the cosmic equivalent of the universe handing her a four-leaf clover and shooting her a lucky star both at the same time.

Breathe, Alex, just breathe.

Tamping down the urge to run, she took a deep breath and called out, "You moved out of position, Whittaker."

Cole's head shot up. A second or so later the rest of him followed as he rocketed out of the seat. "Alex."

She walked toward him, not missing how he stared at her as though she was a Christmas present he'd been dreaming about opening for a very long time. She drew up beside him, and he reached out a hand and touched her shoulder as though testing to see if she was real.

"You said to meet you at Lincoln—*Lincoln*, not Gandhi!"

The two-handed shove she dealt him almost sent him sprawling. The book, her novel, slammed to the ground.

Cole bent to pick it up. "You should have told me." She didn't remember him having fall allergies, but it struck her that his eyes seemed pinkish and more than a little damp.

She tried for a smile. "Who says you're the only one who gets to have a secret life?"

He dropped the book on the bench seat and straightened before her. "What would you say to a moratorium on secret lives, on secrets period?"

Feeling as though he'd just handed her the key to her personal Pandora's Box, Alex swallowed a mouthful of crisp autumn air and reached for her courage. "In that case, the other day you said you loved me. Was that the sex talking or—"

He didn't let her finish. "It wasn't the sex talking. It was me talking. Christ, Alex, I've loved you for such a long time. I more than love you. I'm crazy about you. When I'm around you, I can't see or think straight, I love you so goddamned much. Why do you think I made so many rookie screw-ups in Belize? To be a bodyguard, you have to maintain objectivity, a certain level of emotional detachment. Loving you stripped away any objectivity I had, forget about detachment. The question is can you love me? I'm still the same guy I was yesterday complete with blind spots and warts."

Her mother's words came back to her, only imbued with fresh perspective. *We're all frogs, we all have warts. The best any of us can hope for is to find a fellow frog that will care for us, warts and all.*

She shook her head, not missing how that small gesture had the light in his eyes fading to blackout. "Loving you isn't smart, Cole, it just isn't." She expected him to interrupt and defend himself, only he didn't. "You're pigheaded and egocentric at times and an adrenaline junkie when it comes to the job." After the other day, bringing up his job was the equivalent of pressing on an exposed nerve, and they both knew it.

But Cole kept his cool. "With you on my team, Lex, I can do anything, be anything. I have faith in us, but I need you to believe just a little bit, too. And I need to know you still love me. Even if it's only just a little bit, it's better than nothing. It's a start."

Warm wetness splashed her cheek. Eyes swimming, Alex shook her head. "I don't love you a little. I love you a lot. I love you with my whole heart. And I don't want to lose you again—but I don't want to lose me, either."

"You won't lose me, baby, and I wouldn't dream of trying to clip your wings. I want you to soar, Lex, because as much as I loved you five years ago, I love you ten times more today." He bent and brushed closed-mouth kisses over her forehead, her eyelids and the corners of her mouth.

She opened her eyes and looked beyond his shoulder to the statue of Gandhi smiling down on them. Someone had decked out the famous Indian peace activist in a necklace of pink carnations and stuck a single red rose into his outstretched hand. Captured in mid-stride, he looked like a jolly, geriatric Lothario.

And suddenly she knew that from here on it was going to be all right, really all right. Better than all right, it was going to be pretty wonderful.

He framed her face between his big, warm hands. "Now that we have this love thing squared away, do you think we could settle down to just being happy?"

Alex sniffed. A tissue would be really great right now. "This is finally happening, isn't it? Things are finally working out for us. I can't believe it. I'm so happy, I'm almost afraid."

She slid a hand inside his coat collar, feeling the pulse striking hard and fast alongside his neck.

He rested his forehead against hers. "Don't be. Sure, we're five years behind schedule, but we're getting back on track as of now. I'm going to make you happy, Lex. You might say I'm going to take on making you happy as my life's mission." He captured her hand and kissed her fingers. "Marry me and I swear I'll spend the rest of my life finding new ways to make you happy—in bed and out of it. Think of it as turning the page on a new chapter."

Even wearing heels, she had to rise up on her toes to reach him. It was worth it, though. She wound her arms about his neck and pressed close, wonderfully close as his arms wrapped around her. "After what we've been through, we deserve more than a chapter. This time around we get to write a whole new book."

Epilogue

WATCHING COLE CLIMB DOWN the ladder from painting their former guest bedroom's fourteen-foot ceiling, Alex called up, "We've just had our first official married couple fight. I won, by the way."

He stepped off the last ladder rung and turned to face her. "You call that a fight? It hardly counted as a spat." He had a smudge of daffodil yellow riding the bridge of his nose. More of the same speckled his salt-and-pepper hair.

She rested her folded arms atop the baby bump poking out the front flap of her denim overalls. "Work with me here, will you? It was a fight, all right. I was really pissed when you challenged me on the lamb wallpaper trim. Bears are so last season."

Cole glanced back up at the wallpaper border of dreamy-eyed lambs jumping white picket fences and frolicking in pea-green meadows beneath a canopy of robin's-egg-blue sky and shook his head. "I guess this means the honeymoon is over."

"Guess again."

He swiveled his gaze from the ceiling back to her. "Make-up sex?"

She nodded. "Uh-huh. That is unless you're too tired or I'm too fat or both."

"Baby, I may be tired, but for make-up sex with you, I'd come back from the dead."

She noted how he'd diplomatically declined comment on her weight and smiled. "But what about your back? A little while ago you said it was aching."

"All better now, Scout's honor." He held up a hand palm-out and tried for a solemn look, but the glint in his blue eyes ruined the effect totally.

Laughing, she shook her head, reached up and plucked a chunk of plaster out of his hair. "You were so never a Boy Scout."

He laid his hands on her hips and drew her gently to him. "Yeah, well, that may be true, but, baby, can I ever light your fire." He winked at her.

The cornball line had her laughing so hard that for a few seconds she was afraid she might pee herself, not an unheard-of occurrence these days. Along with sleeping on her stomach, bladder control was something she really, really missed.

They'd spent the past six months restoring an Italianate brownstone in Brooklyn Heights. Friday nights usually involved an informal block party with neighbors, mostly young professional couples and starter families. Over bottles of Sam Adams and bowls of Tex Mex dip, they traded war stories about their respective money pits.

Practically, the location was ideal on any number of levels. With Alex working on her new novel, she could take the subway into Manhattan to meet with her new editor and agent whenever she needed. After considerable discussion with his four business partners, Cole had convinced them they didn't have to choose between keeping Guidepost boutique and growing it global. They could have the best of both worlds. Now Mike, Sal and Jake headed up the Denver office, which was expanding to a more multinational client base, while

Cole and Lester manned a satellite office based out of Manhattan that focused on executive escort. It wasn't always a perfect balance, but it was close to perfect, damned close.

As for Randall, after receiving a copy of Cole's tape, Traxton Biotech's board of directors had convened an emergency closed door meeting and fired him on the spot. Security had shown him the door directly afterward. Rather than stick around for charges to be pressed, he'd fled to Central America, but not before the embezzled money was recovered in full. Who knew, even now he and Tony and Irma Sumatra might be sharing the same patch of beachfront. As far as Alex was concerned, so long as they steered clear of the States—and her and her family—they could have as much tropical "paradise" as they could stand.

Cole glanced over at her. "Race you to the top of the stairs."

She faked a frown. "But I'm pregnant."

He shrugged. "Hey, babe, I play to win, but in this case, I'll be a softie and let you hitch a ride." The next thing she knew, he swung her up into his arms.

Giving herself up to the moment, she wound both arms around his neck and tucked her head beneath his chin. Feeling like Scarlett O'Hara, albeit a very pregnant Scarlett, she let him carry her up the stairs.

Later that afternoon, Cole rolled onto his back and snuggled Alex against him. "I'm the luckiest man in the world." He smoothed a hand over her blossoming belly. The caress met with a tiny kick.

"I know." Smiling, she snuggled closer. "But since I'm the luckiest woman in the world, I guess it kind of balances out."

Cole's chuckle was a low rumble beneath her. "I guess so." He pressed a kiss atop her head.

She lifted her face to look at him. "You know, in another

few months life is going to get pretty crazy around here. It's going to be diapers and bottles and 2:00 a.m. wake-up calls. And they won't be booty calls, either—well, at least not all of them. That's a lot of change to sign up for. No regrets, Special Agent Whittaker?"

Cole didn't hesitate. "Not one."

Though he'd traveled to thirty countries, these days he swore the one place he wanted to be was home with her. Seeing the lazy, contented look he wore on weekends especially, Alex believed him.

"Me, neither." She shifted to get comfortable, for the next thirty seconds at least. "To somebody looking in from the outside, our life might seem kind of boring, but after all the drama we lived through, it's kind of nice just to…well, just to be happy, isn't it?"

He levered himself up on one elbow and leaned over her, his blue eyes, icy no more, beaming down on her. "Yes, Lex, it is nice. I'd say it's pretty damned wonderful."

* * * * *

*Celebrate 60 years of pure reading pleasure
with Harlequin® Books!*

*Harlequin Romance® is celebrating
by showering you with*
DIAMOND BRIDES
*in February 2009.
Six stories that promise to
bring a touch of sparkle to your life,
with diamond proposals and dazzling weddings,
sparkling brides and gorgeous grooms!*

Enjoy a sneak peek at Caroline Anderson's
TWO LITTLE MIRACLES,
*available February 2009
from Harlequin Romance®*

'I'VE FOUND HER.'

Max froze.

It was what he'd been waiting for since June, but now—now he was almost afraid to voice the question. His heart stalling, he leaned slowly back in his chair and scoured the investigator's face for clues. 'Where?' he asked, and his voice sounded rough and unused, like a rusty hinge.

'In Suffolk. She's living in a cottage.'

Living. His heart crashed back to life, and he sucked in a long, slow breath. All these months he'd feared—

'Is she well?'

'Yes, she's well.'

He had to force himself to ask the next question. 'Alone?'

The man paused. 'No. The cottage belongs to a man called John Blake. He's working away at the moment, but he comes and goes.'

God. He felt sick. So sick he hardly registered the next few words, but then gradually they sank in. 'She's got *what?*'

'Babies. Twin girls. They're eight months old.'

'Eight—?' he echoed under his breath. 'They must be his.'

He was thinking out loud, but the P.I. heard and corrected him.

'Apparently not. I gather they're hers. She's been there since mid-January last year, and they were born during the summer—June, the woman in the post office thought. She was more than helpful. I think there's been a certain amount of speculation about their relationship.'

He'd just bet there had. God, he was going to kill her. Or Blake. Maybe both of them.

'Of course, looking at the dates, she was presumably pregnant when she left you, so they could be yours, or she could have been having an affair with this Blake character before…'

He glared at the unfortunate P.I. 'Just stick to your job. I can do the math,' he snapped, swallowing the unpalatable possibility that she'd been unfaithful to him before she'd left. 'Where is she? I want the address.'

'It's all in here,' the man said, sliding a large envelope across the desk to him. 'With my invoice.'

'I'll get it seen to. Thank you.'

'If there's anything else you need, Mr Gallagher, any further information—'

'I'll be in touch.'

'The woman in the post office told me Blake was away at the moment, if that helps,' he added quietly, and opened the door.

Max stared down at the envelope, hardly daring to open it, but when the door clicked softly shut behind the P.I., he eased up the flap, tipped it and felt his breath jam in his throat as the photos spilled out over the desk.

Oh, lord, she looked gorgeous. Different, though. It took him a moment to recognise her, because she'd grown her hair, and it was tied back in a ponytail, making her look younger and somehow freer. The blond highlights were gone, and it was back to its natural soft golden-brown, with a little curl in the end of the ponytail that he wanted to thread his finger through and tug, just gently, to draw her back to him.

Crazy. She'd put on a little weight, but it suited her. She looked well and happy and beautiful, but oddly, considering how desperate he'd been for news of her for the past year—one year, three weeks and two days, to be exact—it wasn't only Julia who held his attention after the initial shock. It was the babies sitting side by side in a supermarket trolley. Two identical and absolutely beautiful little girls.

* * * * *

When Max Gallagher hires a P.I. to find his estranged wife, Julia, he discovers she's not alone—she has twin baby girls, and they might be his. Now workaholic Max has just two weeks to prove that he can be a wonderful husband and father to the family he wants to treasure.

Look for TWO LITTLE MIRACLES
by Caroline Anderson,
available February 2009
from Harlequin Romance®

HARLEQUIN® *Romance*®

This February the Harlequin® Romance series
will feature six Diamond Brides stories featuring
diamond proposals and gorgeous grooms.

Share your dream wedding proposal and you could WIN!

The most romantic entry will win a diamond
necklace and will inspire a proposal in one of
our upcoming Diamond Grooms books in 2010.

In 100 words or less, tell us the most romantic
way that you dream of being proposed to.

For more information, and to enter
the Diamond Brides Proposal contest, please visit
www.DiamondBridesProposal.com

Or mail your entry to us at:

IN THE U.S.: 3010 Walden Ave., P.O. Box 9069, Buffalo, NY 14269-9069
IN CANADA: 225 Duncan Mill Road, Don Mills, ON M3B 3K9

www.eHarlequin.com   HRCONTESTFEB09

REQUEST YOUR FREE BOOKS!

2 FREE NOVELS
PLUS 2
FREE GIFTS!

HARLEQUIN®

Blaze™

Red-hot reads!

You're invited to join our Tell Harlequin Reader Panel!

By joining our new reader panel you will:

- Receive Harlequin® books—they are FREE and yours to keep with no obligation to purchase anything!
- Participate in fun online surveys
- Exchange opinions and ideas with women just like you
- Have a say in our new book ideas and help us publish the best in women's fiction

In addition, you will have a chance to win great prizes and receive special gifts! See Web site for details. Some conditions apply. Space is limited.

To join, visit us at

www.TellHarlequin.com.

COMING NEXT MONTH

#447 BLAZING BEDTIME STORIES Kimberly Raye, Leslie Kelly, Rhonda Nelson
Who said fairy tales are just for kids? Three intrepid Blaze heroines decide to take a break from reality—and discover, to their personal satisfaction, just how sexy happily-ever-afters can be....

#448 SOMETHING WICKED Julie Leto
Josie Vargas has always believed in love at first sight—and once she meets lawman Rick Fernandez, she's a goner. If only he didn't have those demons stalking him....

#449 THE CONCUBINE Jade Lee
Blaze Historicals
Chen Ji Yue has the chance to bring the ultimate honor to her family if she is chosen as one of the new emperor's wives. Of course, first she has to beat out the other three hundred virgins vying for the position. And then she has to stay out of the bed of Sun Bo Tao, the emperor's best friend.

#450 SHE THINKS HER EX IS SEXY... Joanne Rock
24 Hours: Lost
After a very public quarrel with her boyfriend, rock star Romeo Jinks, actress Shannon Leigh just wants to get her life back. But when she finds herself stranded in the Sonoran Desert with her ex, she learns that great sex can make breaking up hard to do.

#451 ABLE-BODIED Karen Foley
Uniformly Hot!
Delta Force operator Ransom Bennett is used to handling anything that comes his way. But debilitating headaches have put him almost out of action. Luckily, his new neighbor, Hannah Hartwell, knows how to handle his pain...and him, too.

#452 UNDER THE INFLUENCE Nancy Warren
Forbidden Fantasies
Sexy bartender Johnny Santini mixes one wicked martini. Or so business exec Natalie Fanshaw discovers, sitting at his bar one lonely Valentine's night. Could a fling with him be a recipe for disaster? Well, she could always claim to be under the influence....